Love
Lies
Dead

Carol Kennedy

ISBN: 9781521248560

DEDICATION

To my wonderful husband, Ian, lovingly referred to as 'Him Indoors'

My first novel. I couldn't have done this without the support of my husband and family. You kept me going when I thought I couldn't do it. Your love and encouragement has been, as always, absolutely brilliant. Thank you.

.

CONTENTS

Chapter One   Page   1

Chapter Two   Page   5

Chapter Three   Page   13

Chapter Four   Page   21

Chapter Five   Page   33

Chapter Six   Page   51

Chapter Seven   Page   55

Chapter Eight   Page   69

Chapter Nine   Page   75

Chapter Ten   Page   107

Chapter Eleven   Page   119

Chapter Twelve	Page	131
Chapter Thirteen	Page	139
Chapter Fourteen	Page	157
Chapter Fifteen	Page	193
Chapter Sixteen	Page	233
Chapter Seventeen	Page	241
Chapter Eighteen	Page	253
Chapter Nineteen	Page	279
Chapter Twenty	Page	289
Chapter Twenty one	Page	297
Chapter Twenty two	Page	305
Chapter Twenty three	Page	

ACKNOWLEDGMENTS

A huge thank you to my two friends Donna and Lindsey
for reading the first draft and encouraging me to continue

CHAPTER ONE

Michael stood in front of the Registrar holding Jenny's hand gazing into her eyes. He'd never seen her look more beautiful than she did today, ready to become his wife. Her hair was drawn back into a chignon with a sprig of gypsophila, decorated with tiny fuchsia and diamond sparkles, set to one side of it nestled in the folds of her hair. She'd managed to find some drop pearl earrings that had a tiny fuchsia coloured ruby where the pearl joined the wire fitment. Michael was wearing a dark blue three-piece suit, with a pale cream shirt that matched the colour of Jenny's dress. His tie was a fuchsia colour to match the flowers Jenny carried in her bouquet and he wore a pale pink rose in his button-hole.

Jenny's dress was in the style of a vintage tea-dress, mid-calf in length with a sweet-heart neckline, and matching silk shoes. She had a fuchsia coloured silk wrap over her shoulders.

The Registrar stood and began the ceremony.

'Michael, will you take Jennifer to be your wife? Will you love her, comfort her; honour and protect her, and forsaking all others, be faithful to her as long as you both shall live?'

Michaels answer of 'I will' was caught up in a gulp as he fought back the tears. How could this beautiful woman be standing there in front of him agreeing to be his wife? He felt truly blessed and extremely lucky.

Jenny gently squeezed his hand to give assurance. He was more nervous about getting married than Jenny thought he would be.

Michael took his wedding vows seriously. He'd had tears in his eyes as he repeated the words from the Registrar.

'I Michael, take you, Jennifer, to be my wife, to have and to hold from this day forward; for better, for worse, for richer, for poorer, in sickness and in health, to love and to cherish, till death us do part.'

His nerves got the better of him as he repeated the words, and he tried to choke back the tears that were forming, his voice wavering. Holding Jenny's left hand in his, he placed the ring on her finger, causing a tear to escape down his cheek.

'Jennifer, I give you this ring as a sign of our marriage. With my body I honour you, all that I am I give to you, and all that I have I share with you.'

They had matching wedding rings, both inscribed with the date of their wedding.

Michael had been in more danger of shedding tears than Jenny had, which endeared him even more to her. It felt like they were the only two people in the room until the Registrar announced them man and wife and the few friends who were there whooped and cheered.

Jenny looked up at Michael with a smile that lit up her face. She felt so happy. She wasn't surprised to see tears in his eyes, she knew he loved her as much as she loved him. He was so handsome, so strong, yet standing in front of the Registrar he showed his vulnerable side.

He had insisted that they spend the night before their marriage apart and had left a small wrapped box on her pillow with a note.

Please open me.

Inside the box, wrapped in pale pink tissue paper was a delicate silver bracelet with the date of their wedding engraved on one side of it, *1st December 2012* and *Jenny, my world, my wife* engraved on the other side. Jenny decided there and then that she would wear it always.

Three years later, Jenny looked down at the bracelet on her wrist, her eyes misted with tears as she took it off and placed it in her jewellery box.

CHAPTER TWO

After trawling around the city, visiting the local hospitals, and after many social media campaigns, Jenny had resigned herself to the fact that Michael had just walked out of her life without even a goodbye. The tenth of December 2014 was a date that had carved itself into her heart as the day she lost her other half.

Michael had gone to work as usual, but just never came home. This one action was so out of character. He always, without fail, told Jenny if he was going to be late or away, and always rang or texted her if it was an unexpected occurrence. It was one of the things that Jenny loved about him, his caring attitude.

She rang his mobile, and found it was turned off. Next, she sent an email which bounced back to her 550:

The email account that you tried to reach does not exist.

Thinking that perhaps she'd punched in the wrong address by mistake, she fired up her laptop to check her account. The laptop took its time going through the start-up procedure. It was only a year old, but it may as well have been hand-cranked.

'Come on, damn you, I'm in a hurry.'

Jenny spoke to the computer as if it would make a difference, it didn't.

She opened her email account and went to the last message she'd sent Michael. It wasn't there. She checked the deleted folder, nothing. She checked the mail box for the last email Michael had sent her, again nothing. Having checked all the possibilities on her account, Jenny sat dazed, staring at the screen. How could there be no emails whatsoever sent between them? It was as if he had never existed. Silent tears ran from her eyes, then a gulp. A pain hit her in the throat, then travelled to the pit of her stomach. For a few minutes, she felt sick and her face felt clammy. Staring at the screen wasn't producing any answers. She didn't know what to do.

'What do people do in these circumstances? What if he's dead, or lying inured somewhere?'

It was now 11.30pm. Jenny knew it would sound daft to tell someone that her husband was missing, that he should have been home a few hours ago, but he never took her for granted. He always took great care to let her know where he was or that he would be late and to expect him at a given time. It wasn't that Michael was controlling, just the opposite, he just didn't want Jenny to worry unnecessarily about him. Michael had never been out this late without telling her and writing it on the calendar.

'The calendar.' She gasped and rushed from the living room to the kitchen.

The calendar hung in its usual place by the kitchen door but there was nothing written against 10 December or the dates either side of it. The last thing written on it was a big heart with *I Love You* written in the middle of it on the first of December. Jenny had smiled when she'd first seen it and written *I love you too* next to it. Jenny turned and leaned against the larder door, dazed, her legs buckled underneath her and she slid to the floor.

'Why aren't you here Michael? Where are you? O God, please be ok, I love you so much and I need you here, right now.'

Her hair stuck to her face where it had come into contact with her tears. She pushed the strands back behind her ears and fished out a crumpled tissue from the pocket in her jeans to blow her nose and wipe away the drying stream of her tears.

From where she sat, Jenny could see down the hall to the front door, her eyes never left it, she wanted to capture the very second he walked in. She woke up with a start. It was dark, cold and she was stiff from sitting on the floor. Her neck ached from being sat in the same position for a couple of hours. Gently rubbing the back of her neck then moving it slowly from side to side to ease the stiffness, she stood up and felt blindly for the kitchen light and switched it on.

'Michael… Michael are you home?'

Jenny ran upstairs calling his name, but there was only silence. It was strange how quiet the house could be with one person in it, yet so alive when they were both there. Opening their bedroom door and turning on the light, Jenny expected to see Michael lying in bed. The duvet was stretched across the bed, the way she'd left it that morning, the bed was empty.

'Of course he's not home, silly, he'd have woken me up as he came in at the very least, and he'd have laughed at my paranoia.'

Jenny fell on the bed, pulled the duvet over her. She pulled Michael's pillow into her arms where she could smell what she could only describe as the essence of Michael, and sobbed till she fell asleep.

When she awoke in the morning, it was grey, cloudy and cold. Jenny stretched out her arm to Michael's side of the bed. It was still empty. She wandered out to the toilet and saw Michael's razor and toothbrush were where he'd left them the previous morning. Tears slid down her face again. Looking in the mirror, a puffy-eyed, wild-haired urchin looked back at her. She looked like she'd slept in her all week, not just the one night. She peeled off her clothes and ran a shower letting the water heat up before stepping under the steaming torrent. The water drowned her tears, the heat of the water refreshing her body but not her mind or her puffy eyes. She stood for some minutes just letting the water pour over her before switching the shower off and stepping out and wrapping herself in her large fluffy towel. Barely dry, she dressed in fresh clothes, jeans, t-shirt and a jumper, combed her hair and ran downstairs. In the kitchen, she switched on the kettle, flung coffee in a mug and went to the living room to retrieve her laptop. Sat at the kitchen table, she looked up the gym where Michael worked. She'd never rung the gym before as Michael was nearly always on the end of his mobile. Jenny wrote the number down on a pad of paper and rang it.

'Good morning, Fitness For You, how can I help you?' came the sing-song voice on the other end.

Jenny pulled a face at the sound of the voice. How could anybody be so flipping happy sounding when her own world was falling down about her. She took a deep breath.

'Er, hello, this is Jenny Black, Michael Black's wife, can you tell me if he's in this morning please?'

'Hello Jenny, I'm sorry but we don't have anyone called Michael working here.'

'Oh, I'm sorry, I must have dialled the wrong number. My apol…' She didn't get to finish the sentence as she was cut off. She checked the number again on the computer, dialled it again and heard the same sing-song voice answering the phone.

'Good morning, Fitness For You, how can I help you?'

'Is this the gym in the High Street or Gerard Road?'

'This is the High Street.'

'Ok, thanks. I've rung the wrong number' Jenny replied, and put the phone down.

It was definitely the gym Michael worked at, so why didn't they know him there? Jenny sat in a stupor, holding her mug of coffee, which had now gone cold. Perhaps she'd got the name of the gym wrong, but having washed Michael's work clothes more times than she could remember, she could envisage the logo without very much effort. She tried ringing Michael's phone again, but there was no response. She tried sending another email and received the same message as before. She dialled her phone again, this time 101 to report a missing person.

'I hope you can help me, I need to report a missing person, my husband that is.'

'Ok, how long has he been missing for?'

'Well I know it sounds daft, but he didn't come home last night. This is just so not Michael. I know there's something wrong.'

The officer who took Jenny's call was sympathetic, and asked her a few questions for a 'safe and well' check, after which he concluded that Michael was not at risk of any harm.

'All I can suggest at the moment, Miss, is that if he hasn't

come home in the next few days, contact the Missing
People Organizations they should be able to help you.'

She thanked him for his help and as she ended the call,
dropped her pen which rolled under the fridge.

'Oh damn, what did you go and do that for?' she scolded
the pen. 'And you've rolled so far under, I can't flippin'
reach you.'

Jenny didn't want to move the fridge, so looked around the
kitchen for a suitable implement to flip it out with. Had it
not been for the fact that the pen had been a gift from
Michael, she would probably have left it where it had rolled.
On the work-surface next to the cooker she saw a spatula.

'Just the job. Come on, you've important work to do,
getting my pen back from under the fridge.'

As she poked the spatula under the fridge and flicked it
back towards her, she successfully not only retrieved her
pen, but a faded piece of paper which turned out to be a
newspaper article, dated 2nd December 2014, about a
Faberge Egg that had been found on a bric-a-brac stall.
Jenny would normally skim read articles like these, but this
one had Michael's writing on it, commenting throughout

the account. He had circled that fact that only 42 of the probable 50 eggs made by Carl Faberge had ever been recovered and that the remaining eight were believed lost or destroyed. He had also circled the information that related to an egg that had recently been bought at an American flea market for approximately £8,000 and was believed to have been sold for a figure in excess of £20 million. One comment Michael had written was *need to find one*. Another comment read, *re-check family history, granny CC spoke about Russian treasure*. Jenny wondered why Michael would have been interested in the article. He'd never mentioned it to her, or remarked on any interest in missing Romanov treasures.

CHAPTER THREE

Jenny Bird (she'd kept her maiden name), was thirty-four years old, blonde, blue-eyed and petite. She had been married to Michael for two years before he had walked out of her life the previous year.

They had met through speed-dating held in a bar in Birmingham. Michael had been the first and only person she chatted with that evening and they hit it off immediately. It was only by chance that Jenny had gone to the speed-dating event. A leaflet had dropped through the letter box with her usual post. The information suggested that this event was for singles who were 30+. It appealed to her. She'd had relationships, but none of them had lasted very long. What tempted her to go was the fact that it was a thirty-minute train journey away from home, so the chances of bumping into someone she'd dated before, would be very remote. So, there she was a week later talking to Michael as if she'd known him all her life. He was seven years older than Jenny and had left the army five years previously having joined up when he was eighteen.

'So what do you do now' Jenny asked.

'When I left the services, I set myself up as a fitness instructor, mostly freelance, but I have a contract with 'Fitness For You' for a limited number of days per year which allows me to take work as a personal trainer whenever I want or need to.'

'Have you got private clients then?'

'Yes, I've got a small number of well-paying clients who book my services around three times a year for a couple of weeks at a time, often abroad, for team building and motivational training. So the time adds up.'

'Wow, that sounds interesting…'

'It was to begin with, but now it's hard to find new programmes to run, especially for the team building events.'

His fitness training showed. He looked like he had a six-pack rippling away under his shirt. Standing at 5' 10", green-eyed with dark brown hair that was trying its best to curl, he was a walking heart-throb, well at least in Jenny's eyes he was.

'Do you have any brothers or sisters?'

'No, I'm an only child. My parents died in a boating

accident when I was young leaving me in the care of my grandmother who passed away last year.'

'I'm sorry to hear that. I'm an only child as well, but my parents are still with us. My grandparents died a few years ago. Have you been married before?'

'No, while I was a serving officer, I hated the thought of someone fretting about me while I was on a tour of duty. Too many of my friends and colleagues have died in service leaving grieving family at home. I've had relationships since leaving the army, but none of them have lasted long.'

This meeting with Jenny soon turned into a whirlwind romance. They met every night for the first three weeks when Michael would bring Jenny a small gift. Sometimes it was a single flower or a bouquet, other times it would be a small box of handmade chocolates, then Michael moved in with her. He continued to spoil her with gifts, not daily, but at least once, every week. Four months later they were married in the town's registry office. Jenny only informed her parents of her nuptials two days before the event. She hadn't wanted a large showy wedding and although her mother was very disappointed that she hadn't had the opportunity to organise a large family wedding, she was overjoyed that her daughter had found someone to love and cherish her, just as she had, and her parents before her.

Michael and Jenny shared the same passion for cryptic crosswords, wine and films, and both had a madcap sense of humour. Their leisure time was spent on the outdoor life, walking, geocaching and orienteering. If they had a walking holiday, Michael always ensured that a 'sit in the sun, do nothing holiday' followed. After they were married, Michael insisted on replacing Jenny's run-down Citroen 2CV with something that would be more reliable. Jenny had been saving up to replace it, but never had quite enough money. He didn't have the heart to tell her that he hated that particular model. It reminded him of a deckchair on wheels. Jenny had chosen a Renault Twingo.

 Life was good, and Jenny couldn't see how it could get any better. December 10, 2014 showed how bad it could get. She tried to carry on as normal, going into work hoping that when she arrived home, Michael would be there. The week before Christmas, her line manager found her in floods of tears and the whole sorry story came tumbling out.

'Jenny, why on earth didn't you tell me when all this first

happened? You must be going through hell.'

'I wanted to Kate, but I didn't know how.'

'I'm going to put you on compassionate leave for however long you need. Why don't you go home to your parents for a while?'

'No, I'll be alright…' The tears started again.

'Jenny, you need time to process all of this. As your friend and your manager, I'm telling you to go home. I'll keep in contact and you come back to work when you feel ready.'

It had taken three months before Jenny felt able to cope with returning to work.

CHAPTER FOUR

Jenny walked through the automatic doors of the supermarket, that opened with an audible swoosh. The store was busy with parents trying to control excited children, people pushing trolleys without any thought of where they were going and others having a discussion about the cost of Christmas crackers. As she picked up a basket, Jenny tried to remember what it was she had come in for.

'Croissants, bread, chocolate and…' perhaps it would come to her as she walked up and down each aisle – a system she'd used before with varying levels of success.

Coming across the alcohol aisle, Jenny remembered that she was going to see if there were any packs of whisky miniatures for her father; this wasn't the forgotten item, but it was something she intended on buying. Scanning the shelves, there were no items that grabbed her attention, though as she walked past the gin bottles, she did notice one of her favourite gins, not usually for sale in this store, with the bonus of it being on offer. She added it to her basket – well it would have been rude not to, she decided.

In the back-ground she could hear Christmas music being played and for a moment, it brought a heavy feeling to her breathing reminding her that Michael wasn't here to enjoy Christmas with her. Blocking out the sound, Jenny continued through the various aisles and unable to recall what else she needed, proceeded to the check-out. As she approached the self-service till, a lady crashed her trolley into the back of Jenny's ankle.

'Ouch' cried Jenny and turned around.

'Oh, sorry love, I can't get used to these things. You forget how long they are don't you? Hope I didn't hurt you.'

'No worries, it's easily done, there's no damage.'

She tried not to limp as she spotted an empty till. She passed each item over the scanner and placed it in her shopping bag. When it came to the bottle of gin, the automatic voice called out:

'Please wait for assistance.'

'These machines need some sort of age recognition on them' Jenny said to the sales assistant.

'Yes, they do' the assistant replied, as if she hadn't heard it a hundred times a day for the last five years.

Walking through the foyer back to the car park, a small brass band were now joyously playing *Jingle Bells*.

'Grrr, there is no snow', she muttered to herself, 'don't they know it isn't actually a Christmas song…arrrrgghhh it was written for Thanksgiving and that was a few weeks ago.'

Jenny had come across this information watching a quiz show on television and was intrigued by the information.

'Why can't they play Christmas Carol's if they must play anything?'

Though even *In The Bleak Mid-Winter* wasn't going to cut it with her, 13°C, bright sunshine, nothing like the weather one would expect three days before Christmas.

As she reached her car, Jenny turned around. It felt like she was being watched, but as she scanned the area around her, she couldn't see anyone. This had happened a lot recently. The feeling that someone was watching her, yet when she turned around, there was nobody there. It sent a shiver down her back. A few times, she thought she'd seen Michael, but friends said this was a normal phenomenon when a loved one had gone. There was no-one walking to or from their cars in the area. Jenny fumbled with the lock on the car door, pushed her shopping onto the passenger seat as she got in, locked the door and howled.

'How long is this supposed to last' she cried, banging the steering wheel with both hands. 'It's been one miserable year and I don't feel any different. Michael where are you, I need you to come back home.'

She sat in the car until her tears subsided, wiped her face and looked in the mirror on the sun visor.

'Get a grip Jen. If he was going to come home, you know he'd have done it by now.'

A couple, from the car parked next door, knocked on the window.

'Are you alright, dear?'

Jenny wound her window down a couple of inches.

'Yes, thank you, I was a bit upset, but I'm alright now.'

Feeling more composed, she gave her face a final look in the mirror, no smudged mascara or eyeliner, because she'd forgotten to put it on. Pulling her fingers through her hair as a make-shift comb, she slid the cover over the mirror, started the engine, checked all around her and reversed out of the parking space. Almost immediately a car hooted it's horn at her and glancing in the rear-view mirror she saw a bright red Fiesta with a driver holding his hands up in the air in despair. 'Sorry' she mouthed and drove off.

Jenny lived in what was once a small village, but now, through building on waste ground and redundant fields, the population numbers decreed that it was a small town. Her house, which was built in the 1950s in the older part of the village, was semi-detached with a brick porch which gave protection from the elements to anyone stood waiting to be let in. The front door opened onto a hall with space on the left for a coat rack and the stairs. Down the hall to the right were a living room and a dining room. To the left, the space under the stairs had been made into a downstairs toilet. The kitchen was straight ahead. Upstairs the first room was the bathroom. There were three bedrooms leading off a generous landing. There were bay windows at the front looking out on a small front garden which when Jenny moved in was a patch of grass. She managed to persuade her dad to replace it with gravel which extended the drive space. At the rear of the property there was an enormous garden, half of which was laid to lawn, while the rest was a ridiculously overgrown vegetable patch. A shed sat in a space between two halves housing summer garden furniture.

Arriving home, Jenny found that the postman had been most generous in his delivery, nine envelopes all looking like Christmas cards. Picking them up off the mat, she shut the door behind her and walked down the hall to the kitchen, switching on the kettle before taking off her jacket and hanging it on the back of a kitchen chair. Five minutes later she was sat at the kitchen table opening her post. The first card was from an old school friend, Julia with a note telling her that she'd moved and here was her new address. The second card didn't have a stamp on it, but was addressed as if it should have done.

'Oh dear, I wonder who managed to put this in the post.'

When she opened the envelope, she was showered with glitter from the front of the card. She opened the card to see who had sent it, but there was no name just a string of numbers.

26.3   *71.123*   *71.526* ~~*not*~~   *97.123*

It didn't make sense. Jenny closed the card and studied the picture, it was an olde worlde village scene of black and white houses, a spired church in the background, and snow and glitter everywhere. She looked at the back of the card, to see if it gave any hint of where it was supposed to be, but it just said, *from the mixed group of nonets – printed in Great Britain*. The verse inside read simply

Warmest wishes at Christmas and always

Let it snow, let it snow, let it snow

Somebody was having a laugh. It amused her, considering the amount of glitter that had fallen out of the envelope, and perplexed her at the same time.

The next two cards were from friends, promising that they must meet up in the next year. The following card brought a feeling of déjà vu when another shower of glitter cascaded over the kitchen table. The picture on the front of the card was a similar village view to the first glitter card, but showed more of the church with the houses beyond it. The verse inside was the same, as was the back of the card. Again, nobody had signed it, but had written

10+6+5+5+22+11=V

Why on earth would someone send two similar cards with numbers and no signature? Jenny picked up the envelope, another one without a stamp. Perhaps they had been hand delivered, but they were in the middle of the pile that the postman had dropped through the letter box.

Having finished her coffee, Jenny went upstairs to finish her packing. She was going to her parents for Christmas, which she was glad about, as it meant she wouldn't sit at home moping about what she and Michael could have been doing. Just as she was closing up her travel case, the door-bell rang. Running down the stairs Jenny could see someone on the other side wearing a high-viz jacket, her heart started pounding, what if it was the police come to tell her they'd found Michael's body?

'Oh for heaven's sake Jen, get a grip, if it was the police, there would be two of them and they would not be wearing a high-viz jacket' she scolded herself.

She opened the door tentatively and was relieved to see it was a delivery driver with a package that would not have fitted through the letter-box. After thanking him and closing the door, Jenny inspected the package. It was addressed to her, but she couldn't remember ordering anything that she hadn't already received. Pulling the tear-away strip on the back of the package, a wrapped parcel fell out with a slip of paper bearing the message:

For Christmas Day, **Not** *to be opened before-hand.*

'A Christmas present, how lovely.'

At that moment, the phone rang, as she answered it, the caller put the phone down. Dialling 1471, Jenny heard the recorded voice saying

'You were called at 14.22 hours, the caller withheld their number.'

She concluded that it must have been one of those rogue marketing companies. She'd had a number of calls lately telling her that her broadband was being used by other people or that her computer had a virus; all spam calls. The phone call did remind her that she needed to ring her parents to tell them what time her train was arriving the next day. The answer-phone picked up at her parents' home and she heard the delightful message concocted by both parents saying

'We are unable to take the call right now as we are probably up to our knees in mud in the garden, so please leave a message we can listen to when we come in to clean our wellies.'

A new message. They never ceased to amaze her with their range of announcements. One that had made her giggle last year was that they probably had their arm up a cow's bum helping it to give birth. She could just imagine them doing that. Another favourite was that they were busy stuffing a scarecrow. The best of it was, her parents had put in a tenant farmer five years ago and were living the high life, taking holidays whenever they felt the urge. She left a message

'Hi it's Jen, I'm getting the 12.05 train which should get in at 1.45pm. See you tomorrow. Bye.'

Having brought her travel bag downstairs, Jenny made herself a sandwich and a mug of coffee before settling herself in the living room to watch a film. At first, she couldn't decide between A White Christmas or A Wonderful Life but eventually opted for the latter as it was in black and white and matched her mood. The film, as always, had her in tears, but this time there were no comforting arms from Michael, arms that would pull her into him and hold her in a warm embrace with large gentle hands stroking her hair and that soft mellow voice telling her she was loved. The reminder that Michael wasn't there, caused more tears.

CHAPTER FIVE

Jenny boarded the train at mid-day, found her reserved seat and put her travel bag on the overhead rack. Settling herself into her seat, she checked her mobile for any messages, and plugged in her earphones to listen to some music. Across the aisle and two rows down, she could see what could only be described as a hippy from the 1960s. A tall chap, looking at the length of his legs protruding from under the table into the aisle, that showed a pair of well-worn converses, so well-worn that one of them had a hole in the sole. His jeans were light blue denim, with the obligatory tears in the knee, a tie-dyed t-shirt spread over a paunched stomach and a waistcoat. His long hair hung over his face like a veil. All he needed was a flower and John Lennon style glasses and he'd have the whole lot, thought Jenny to herself. She made herself laugh thinking of a song her mother liked playing 'I'm just sitting watching flowers in the rain…' This thought confirmed her music choice for the journey and she dialled through her collection to find *sounds of the sixties*. Jenny had inherited a love of the music from the 1950s and 1960s from her parents. They were songs that you could sing along to, rather than the modern-day rapping. The man didn't move for the whole journey, fast asleep he appeared oblivious to everyone around him.

The train arrived on time and as she disembarked, Jenny could see her mother waiting for her on the other side of the ticket barrier. They waved at each other and Jenny was soon enveloped in a huge hug from her mother, this turned on the emotional tap and tears slid down her face, causing her to gulp.

'It's ok love, it's only natural, it's only been a year, and you are doing brilliantly.'

'Thanks mum, I know, it's just that sometimes it all creeps up on me. I'm ok.'

As they drove home, small flakes of snow started falling, making it feel much more like Christmas. As the car made its way up the hill in the village, the snow started falling heavier and she could feel the tyres trying to get traction on the slippery surface. Jenny's father greeted them at the door with a warm smile and an even warmer hug, which did nothing for the emotional tap that was still dripping.

'Come on in love, I've just lit a fire and there's some coffee brewing to go with the shortbread your mother made this morning, just don't tell her that there are a couple of pieces missing,' her father winked at her and carried her bag inside.

Coming home was always lovely, like she'd never been away, and Jenny settled herself into what she had always considered 'her chair', a deep seated, high-backed chair in pale pink and green chintzy fabric, with broad arms that you could safely balance a plate on, and cushions so soft they hugged you. With her legs tucked up underneath her, Jenny nursed a mug of fresh coffee and nibbled on a couple of fingers of shortbread. Sitting in front of the log fire that looked like it already had a yule log on it, Jenny felt the emotional tap turn off, for now at least. As she sat staring at the fire, her father handed her a parcel.

'This arrived for you yesterday.'

'Really? Nobody knows I'm here. Is it from you and mum?'

'No love. Go on, open it up, perhaps it will say who it's from inside.'

Opening the package, a cryptic crossword book landed on her lap with a label that read simply

enjoy X

Jenny flipped the pages of the book in case there was another piece of paper or indication of who had sent it, but there was nothing. Perhaps it was one of her friends from work who she might have mentioned she was going home for the holiday period, but other than that, Jenny could think of no-one else who would know, and surely, they would have put their name on the label?

The evening was spent in front of the fire watching the television and chatting about how Jenny's work was going and how the new tenants of the farm were settling in. Since Jenny's parents had decided to move into Rose Cottage and have tenants in at the farm, the first family had moved out and a single man moved in. Jenny teased her parents that they worked them too hard.

Drawing the curtains the next morning showed a wonderful white, crisp vista. It made her want to run outside and stomp through the virgin snow like she had done as a young child, but the aroma of breakfast being cooked in the kitchen put that thought on hold. Reaching the kitchen, Jenny saw a full English breakfast laid out for the three of them.

'You look like you need a good meal inside you love, and as it's Christmas, it's the perfect excuse for a good breakfast.'

Jenny laughed. 'I do eat, you know, and I am looking after

myself. Have you got a pair of boots I can borrow I forgot to bring mine and I need to go for a walk after that feast?' She helped herself to another slice of toast. An hour later she was bundled up in her coat, scarf and gloves and a pair of wellington boots a size too big, so she'd put on an extra pair of socks.

The village her parents lived in, and where Jenny herself had grown up in, was Wartlington. A small rural village on the border of Staffordshire and Derbyshire. It had a farm, that had been in her father's family for a number of generations, a church, small infant school, a couple of shops, cottages that lined both sides of the aptly named Church Hill, and a pub which backed on to the garden of her parent's cottage. It was an old coaching inn, complete with gates on both sides to allow coaches to enter and exit. The main building was typical black and white, wattle and daub that took on a grey tinge in the winter months when vehicles splashed mud up from the road onto the walls. The old stables had been demolished a long time ago, mainly because they had fallen down due to neglect. The space was now a car-park, which was rarely empty during opening hours.

All the housing was thatched cottages, with names such as

Bottom Cottage, Church Hill Cottage, School Cottage, Lavender Cottage, Lupin Cottage and The Old Bakery. Some names had been obscured by ivy and other plants. All buildings had a well or water pump, an echo back to the days when there was no plumbed in water, just what was available from the spring that ran under the houses.

Her parents lived in Rose Cottage, referred to by the locals as 'the Bird House'. It was a typical 'chocolate box' cottage with white-washed walls, an overhanging thatch roof, with windows that looked like they were set into the roof. Jenny's bedroom was one of the rooms at the front of the house looking out across Church Hill to the vicarage. Part of the ceiling sloped down towards the floor making it difficult to stand up straight in places and like the rest of the cottage, was decorated beautifully and sensitively, evoking the essence of a time gone by. The downstairs windows were all surrounded by climbing roses which in the summer provided the most beautiful pink and yellow delicate roses that gave off the most gorgeous scent. The front door was a solid oak door with black painted strapping and the front garden was laid out with a border under the windows and each side of the crazy paving path.

The shops which were well stocked with grocery items,

were also thatched and with white-washed walls, were in Church Lane which ran along the top of the village, set across the road from the pub. Whilst one shop contained a butcher and a small fishmonger, the other had a small haberdashery. Further along the lane and diagonally opposite Wartlington Dale Farm was an old Priory dating from before 1470 and appeared to have survived the Reformation. It was a Grade I listed building and belonged to her father, who often received requests to sell it, but Jenny's father wouldn't give way. It was not for sale at any price. Jenny used to play in the Priory with her school friends in the village, but hadn't been in the property for at least fifteen years.

Jenny's walk took her past the pub, across the road, past the shops, down to the corner of the old Priory and Farm, along the bridleway at the side of the farm and round to the bottom of Church Hill. When she got home, having walked up the steep hill, her cheeks were red, her nose cold and a mulled wine was waiting for her.

Christmas Eve saw the usual visit to Midnight Mass. The snow seemed to make it magical and mysterious, and the street lights reflection on the snow, sparkled and glistened. There were footprints showing villagers had walked up the hill and the closer to the church the more footprints there were. It seemed very lonely sitting in the church without Michael at her side, even though she was with her parents. Jenny received several commiseration type smiles and left the church during the last hymn to avoid the ongoing pitying conversations that she'd endured throughout the last year. Christmas day came and went with turkey dinner and exchange of gifts in the afternoon. Snow had steadily fallen over the day and Boxing Day morning was spent watching movies and drinking mulled wine accompanied by shortbread.

'Mum, did you find any more letters from my great, great, grandmother or more information on the family tree?'

Two years ago, she had found a letter in a book of French poetry that had belonged to her great, great, grandmother. The book had been sitting in the bookshelf in the living room. Jenny remembered Michael being surprised when she'd read it out loud, translating it from the written French to English. She explained that it came from having French great, great, grandparents and that each generation had been brought up speaking French and English.

'No, to be honest, I haven't really looked, but there might

be something in the trunk down in the cellar, or there might be something stored in the attic.'

'Is the cellar the best place to store items like that? Surely it's damp down there.'

'No love, it's fine. It's how I occupied myself when your mother came to stay with you. I spent the early spring turning it into my den. It seemed only fair as your mother has commandeered part of the attic for a craft room. Come on, I'll show you what I've been doing down there.'

Jenny's mother smiled and raised her eyes upwards. 'I'm surprised it's taken him this long to get round to showing you. All visitors generally don't get across the threshold before being herded down there. But I have to admit, he has done a good job of it.'

The cellar was wood-panelled throughout and looked very much like a gentlemen's club, complete with a bar, carpeted floor, and, as Jenny very much expected, a dart board and soft leather lounge chairs. In the far corner was a jukebox which on closer inspection contained records of all her father's favourite music.

'So what do you do down here dad, apart from listen to

your music and drink?'

'Well about once a month me, Derek from across the road, George and Steve from down the hill get together and have a darts match, a bit of a chin-wag, you know, putting the world to rights. Your mum can't hear us upstairs, so she's quite happy. The trunk is over in this corner' her father pointed to the opposite side of the bar. 'I'll pull it away from the wall so you can open it properly without any fear of it decapitating yourself... There you go, I'll leave you to it. Help yourself to anything from the bar and make yourself comfortable. Oh and don't forget to leave payment for your drink' he joked as he went back upstairs.

Jenny looked all around her. Never in a million years would you guess it was a cellar. Her father had done a fantastic job, it was bright enough, cosy, luxurious and yes, even warm. She walked behind the bar and investigated the various bottles. Under the counter, there was a small fridge which contained small tins of lemonade and tonic water, a few lagers and in the small icebox, there were even ice-cubes and slices of lemon and lime. He'd thought of everything. Jenny chose a gin and tonic with ice and a slice and placed the glass on the coffee table making sure she used a coaster. She then turned her attention to the trunk.

The trunk looked very old and well-travelled. She wondered which family member had owned it. Everything inside it was in large plastic bags, five of which felt soft, like clothing, while another held something hard, like shoes, which on closer inspection were two pairs of black leather laced shoes with punched leather decoration. There was a hat box, which, when Jenny opened it, held the most delightful olive-green broad-brimmed hat with a sort of ribbon around the crown and an ostrich feather. Nestled inside that, separated by a couple of sheets of tissue paper, was a very simple light grey cloche type hat with a pale apricot coloured band around its middle. Thinking back through fashion history, Jenny estimated that they must be from the 1900s.

She opened one of the bags of what she presumed was clothing. All items were very neatly wrapped in white tissue paper. She found a long black skirt and a black blouse with what could only be described as mutton sleeves, a fashion that was alive and kicking in the 1890s. There was a smaller bag with these items that contained two starched white pinafores. They had very delicate white lace edging the bib part and a pocket on the skirt. When Jenny looked more closely at the blouse, the sleeves were broderie anglaise. It could only be a maid's uniform, but it was beautiful and must have been expensive to purchase at the time. One of the other bags contained exactly the same uniform while the other two bags contained the uniform in white.

The last bag was heavy, and on opening it, Jenny found a mid-leg length woolen coat with a fur collar, something that would definitely keep the cold out. A small bag had fallen out from between the larger bags, it contained three of some sort of headdress. Jenny picked one of them up and wandered over to the bar mirror where she could see how it might have been worn. She pulled her hair up to the top of her head with one hand and sat the headdress on top of it. It had a sort of lace flower from which a short length of veil lace fell, just above her shoulders. The household that this maid had worked in must have been very grand.

At the bottom of the trunk, there was a black lidded box which was awkward to lift out. It wasn't large or too heavy, just at the bottom in the corner where Jenny could not grab hold of it. She climbed into the trunk to pick the box up and rested it on the corner of the trunk while she scrambled back out. She carried it across to the coffee table and set it down. Before opening the box, Jenny sat in one of the chairs and took a sip of her drink. Having seen the maids uniform, she wasn't sure what to expect in the box.

Taking a generous gulp of her drink, Jenny took the lid off the box, or rather she tried to take the lid off. It took a lot of coaxing, pushing the lid along its length and along the other side, and on the third-time round, it came off with a pop. Inside the box was a bundle of letters tied in a ribbon, hopefully the letters she was looking for, a few books, a small box, which Jenny hoped wouldn't be as troublesome to open, a fountain pen, a small bottle containing a miniscule amount of ink and a small heavy object wrapped in tissue paper.

She opened the small box first to find something wrapped in the same white tissue paper that the clothing was wrapped in. She opened it very carefully, having set it on the coffee table in case it was breakable, and in case she dropped it. As she unwrapped each layer, the most exquisite chatelaine appeared. The chains which were suspended from an ornate clasp, appeared to be gold and at the end of each chain was an object. There was a tiny pair of scissors, a thimble, a couple of small keys, a small pencil, ivory sheet, a pen knife, and two small cases, one holding sewing needles and the other two very slender cotton reels with white cotton and black cotton. This was the ultimate maid's tool bag, wearable whilst doing her duties. Jenny wrapped the chatelaine very carefully and placed back in the small box.

Turning her attention to the small object wrapped in similar tissue paper, Jenny took another generous gulp of her drink. Not knowing what to expect after viewing the chatelaine, she was amazed to find a small sculpted bird. She knew exactly what it was as she had what she could only presume was its twin, given to her as a christening gift. A gold salt in the shape of a wren sitting on a nest. Lifting the bird off its nest should reveal a sumptuous deep blue ceramic dish but like the black box before, it, the two halves were not eager to part company. As she moved the wren from her hand back to the table, Jenny heard a sound from inside it that indicated there was something in the salt beside the ceramic dish. She tried to open it again, without success. She wrapped the little bird up and placed it on the table. Sitting back in the chair and clutching her drink, Jenny pondered on why the two birds had been separated and why she had one as a christening gift.

'Jenny, do you want a coffee?' her mother called downstairs.

'Oh, yes please, I'll be up in a couple of minutes.'

Jenny drained her glass and took it over to the bar where

she found a small sink. Having washed the glass, she put it away, and noticed a small note pad and pencil, so quickly drew a smiley face on it and left it on top of the bar, her payment.

Jenny put the clothing bags back in the trunk, and returned upstairs carrying the black box.

'Dad I couldn't find the light switch, so the lights are still on'.

'Don't worry they have a motion sensor fitted, so if they don't detect any movement after ten minutes, they switch off automatically, just like they switch on immediately if they detect a movement. Clever stuff, eh?'

'Have either of you looked through the trunk?

'No, one of those things we haven't got round to. It belonged to your great, great, grandmother. The trunk has been down in the cellar for as long as I can remember. Your mother put all the items in plastic bags, to try and keep them safe and help preserve them.'

'You should see some of these items. There's a second wren salt, like the one I've got.

'Goodness, I didn't realise there were two of them. The one you have Jenny has been handed down from each generation. It goes to the first born of the next generation, so when and if you have your own children, you'll pass it on to your first-born.'

'It was your fathers, and his fathers before him. A family heirloom, so to speak.'

'There is also this chatelaine, it is exquisite. It looks like it was well used.'

'It's beautiful, I could do with something like this, myself.' Jenny's mother laughed.

'There are some letters which I'm hoping are the ones I was looking for and books as well.'

'Take them back with you Jenny, you'll have more time to look at them. I've had a quick look for the family tree, but I can't lay my hands on it, but as soon as I find it, I'll post it to you.'

The following morning, Jenny's mother took her back to the station and said she'd ring her the following weekend. The black box was safely stowed in her travel case, making it slightly heavier than it had been. She had trouble lifting it up onto the luggage rail, but was helped by an older man who was passing by looking for his seat. Having thanked him for his help, she sat down and opened the book of cryptic crosswords she'd received at her parents' home. She must remember to ask her colleagues which one of them sent it. She tried to concentrate on the puzzle, but another passenger in the carriage was engaged in an argument with the gentleman who had helped her with her luggage.

'I don't care if you reserved this seat or not, I've paid for my ticket, I've found a seat, and here I'm staying. There's another seat down there, go sit.'

He had what looked like a black eye and a few days beard growth, and sported a well-formed beer-belly. Jenny could only imagine he'd got his black eye by picking the wrong person in an argument.

The helpful gentleman replied that the seat was facing the wrong direction, which was why he'd reserved his seat in the first place.

'Tough cookies' the objectionable passenger replied.

The spare seat was next to Jenny and she indicated that he

could sit there.

'Thank you. I won't take up your offer. I can't face this way when I'm travelling, it tends to make me feel ill. I'll stand out by the doors until a seat becomes available.'

Jenny stared at the objectionable passenger and shook her head. He responded by blowing her a kiss and winking. Jenny scowled back and turned her attention back to her puzzle book.

CHAPTER SIX

Jenny unlocked her front door at 2pm, grateful to be back home. She loved her parents dearly, but there was only so much coffee she could drink in one day. They seemed to have no sooner finished one cup than they were brewing the next. She placed her bag in the hallway ready to take upstairs next time she went up, and went to the kitchen, to make a coffee. She smiled to herself thinking of the irony. As she waited for the kettle to boil, she went to the living room, as she looked around, something didn't feel right. Nothing looked out of place, but she couldn't put her finger on it. Thinking perhaps it was her imagination, she went back to the kitchen to finish making her drink.

She came back to the living room and turned the television on to the 24-hour news channel to see what was going on in the world. As she sat down to watch, she noticed that her post was on the coffee table. It wasn't the post she received before she left to go to her parents, she'd opened that, it was what would have been delivered after she left and she always took it through to the kitchen. She thought back to everything she'd done when she got home, and picking up the post was not one of them. She went cold and her hand started to tremble, someone had been in the house while she was away. Putting down her coffee, she tip-toed out to the hall and listened at the dining room door for any sound. Nothing. She opened the door as quietly as she could, and peered round the it. Everything was as it should be. Next, Jenny went to the stairs trying to remember which step creaked when it was stood on, oh yes, third from the bottom. She put her foot on the first step and changed her mind. What if there was someone up there?

She went to the kitchen, picked up her mobile and turned to her knife rack, chose a paring knife and returned to the stairs. Her heart was pounding in her chest as she counted under her breath the number of stairs.

'One, two, miss the third, four, five…'

Reaching the landing she looked about and saw all the doors were closed, just as she'd left them. She listened outside each door before peering inside the room, each one ok. Perhaps, she thought, she had picked up the post when she came in, but she knew she hadn't. Someone had been in the house, but there was no sign of a break in. She thought about calling the police, but could imagine their faces as she told them somebody had been in her house, put her post on the coffee table, not taken anything, and left.

'Come on Jen, get a grip, you must have picked up the post and put it on the coffee table, that all there is to it.'

She drank her coffee and went to the kitchen, something stronger was needed, so she sacrificed a large G&T. As she passed the kitchen table, Jenny noticed the wrapped present that had arrived before she left for her parents sitting underneath the pile of Christmas cards. She picked it up and returned to the living room. Opening the package, she was pleasantly surprised to see a book of Shakespeare's Sonnets, a book she had always meant to buy, but had never got around to. She was absolutely delighted, but there was no clue as to who had sent it. That was two books she had received in the post from heaven knows who. Enthralled, she spent the next hour flipping through the book reading different poems. She turned to number 116,

Let me not to the marriage of true minds

Admit impediments. Love is not love

Which alters when it alteration finds,

Or bends with the remover to remove:

Oh no; it is an ever-fixed mark...

Tears slowly ran down her cheeks, it was the reading that she and Michael insisted that they have at their wedding even though it was in the registry office. She read the rest, smiling through her tears at the memory of her wedding day. 'Michael, wherever you are, I love you, and I always will'.

CHAPTER SEVEN

Jenny worked at the library in the main town. All the surrounding villages now merged with it making it a large conglomeration without any specific borders. The building itself was red brick with black brick edging around the doors and windows. The library took up three floors while the basement was where new stock was put until it found its way to the shelves, repairs were made and archive material was kept.

The town itself was built in the Regency period and most buildings were on a central road that on a map, looked like the backbone of an animal, with ribs running off it at regular intervals. The town's hotel was on the main road and boasted the likes of Charles Dickens and Queen Victoria as having been guests.

Jenny usually walked to work in the mornings and caught the bus home in the late afternoon.

Two days after her Christmas break, Jenny arrived home from work, to find a letter from her mother.

Hello darling, I found the family tree, and have enclosed it. There isn't much of it I'm afraid. It's one of those works in progress that I'll get round to finishing one day, though your father thinks pigs will fly first, ha ha. Hope you had a good return to work, I'll ring you at the weekend. Love mum xx

The enclosed paper was a very brief outline of the family tree.

Parents:

Philippe Bird (Oiseau) born 1962

married Eloise Graham 1981

↓

Grandparents:

Albert Bird (Oiseau) born 1942

 married Eve Marchant 1961

(both died in a car accident in 2004)

↓

Great grandparents:

Philippe Bird (Oiseau) born 1922 (died 1944 in the war)

married Gabrielle Petit 1938 (died 1963)

↓

Great, great grandparents:

Etienne Osieau born 1892 (died 1947)

married Genevieve Rosseau 1920 (died 1973)

Her mother had written a further note on the paper.

*Your great, great, grandparents had their surname changed when
they came to England. I'm not sure why, there must be a reason.
The family name has been Bird since then. As you know Oiseau
means bird, so it's sort of understandable. Not the easiest word to
pronounce if you don't know French, and I suppose it stopped people
asking how to say it and what it meant.*

Jenny hadn't prepared anything for her meal that evening,
and decided to have a take-away. She went upstairs and
changed out of her work clothes, and noticing the black
box she'd brought back from her parents, picked it up
and carried it downstairs. She left it in the living room
while she went out to the local shops, returning 15

minutes later with a sweet and sour chicken with fried rice, that would easily feed two people. Some habits were hard to break. She waited until she'd finished eating before opening the box.

Jenny opened the tissue wrapped books first, leaving the letters till last. The first book was *Les Misérables* by Victor Hugo, printed in French, the second was a copy of Charles Dickens' *A Tale of Two Cities*, printed in English, the third book was *The Count of Monte Cristo* by Dumas and the fourth book was Jane Austen's *Pride and Prejudice*. Whoever these books had belonged to, they were well thumbed editions. She lifted each of them to her nose. There was something about the smell of old books that she loved. At the library, she and her colleagues all confessed that it was something they did, but not in public. It was like being in a secret society.

Having looked in awe at the book collection, Jenny turned her attention to the bundle of letters. She carefully undid the ribbon, a faded red velvet, and set it to one side. She'd brought the original letter downstairs with her and reread it first.

10 Octobre 1921

Notre cher Geneviève (Our Dear Genevieve)

It was so joyous to see you and Etienne, you seem so happy together and the news that you are to have your own family is wonderful. We are pleased to know that you have purchased the farm you wanted and we heartedly accept your invitation to come and live with you. We are neither of us getting any younger and farming is such hard work these days. We will be arriving at the end of November.

Cecile is married to a young English gentleman who she met on the boat last time she came to see you. He seems to be a nice young man, and she loves him very much. They will be living in England too, so it makes sense for us to be with you.

We will bring all of your letters with us, they are a wonderful telling of your life in Russia which you will be able to share with your children. We look forward to seeing you very soon. Your loving mother and father

Jenny reached for the family tree that her mother had sent her. Genevieve and Etienne were her great, great grandparents and Genevieve had lived in Russia. She turned to the pile of letters. Some were not legible, as if they had been dropped in water, but they appeared to be in date order. Jenny started reading the first letter.

5 Août 1914

Ma chère mère et mon père (My dear Mother and Father)

Nous étions à Londres quand on nous annonça que la guerre avait éclaté. (We were in London when it was announced that war had broken out.) Her Imperial Majesty said we should go home as soon as possible. So, no sooner had we arrived here and unpacked, than we were repacking.

We reached Berlin, but the authorities refused our train to travel onwards to the Russian Border. We managed to return via Denmark and Finland and the Dowager Empress has set up home at Yelagin Palace as it is closer to St Petersburg. A week later, we learned that the city has been renamed Petrograd...

The next page was missing

...Once again, I have been blessed with a gift from Her Imperial Majesty – a pair of salts in the shape of wrens. I believe they are made of gold, but I am not sure. Equally I am not sure what I will do with them, they are very grand for a farm table.

She is very generous, the jewellery she has given me in the past year is very beautiful. I dare not wear it, in case I lose it.

I will write again soon

Your loving daughter

Genevieve

Jenny sat staring at the letter. If she had read this correctly, then the wren salts, were from the Russian Imperial Family and would undoubtedly be gold.

'Oh my goodness, this is incredible. My great, great, grandmother worked in Russia for the Dowager Empress, mother of Tsar Nicholas II. She saw first-hand all that history as it happened. Wow! I can understand how the salts would have looked out of place on a provincial farm table.'

She went upstairs to her bedroom and fetched down the wren salt that she had on her dressing-table. Setting it on the coffee table in front of her, she carefully unwrapped the wren that had sat in the trunk for goodness knows how many years. Sitting side by side, they looked incredible. It was hard to distinguish which one had been in her possession all her life, and which one had lain hidden in the trunk.

The next few letters were hard to read, and the parts that were legible spoke of the Dowager Empress and how kind she was. Jenny continued through the pile, reading the ones that were least damaged.

30 Novembre 1916

Ma chère mère et mon père

I hope you are both well, I miss you so much. Her Imperial Highness has attended the marriage of her daughter, the Grand Duchess Olga to Nikolai Kulikovsky. Not many people were there, even His Imperial Highness Czar Nicholas did not attend his sister's wedding...

...In other news, Her Imperial Highness continues to try to get Rasputin removed from the grip of the Imperial Family. The Czar says nothing while Czarina Alexandra tries to convince everyone who will listen of his holiness and healing properties...

...Madame does not like Rasputin, she thinks he is trying to control the Czar and...

... continues to serve with Russia's Red Cross and perseveres with her social life as best she can under the circumstances of war...

...I have a new hair comb. It was one of a pair, but the teeth got broken on one, and Madame will only consider wearing pairs of

combs, so lucky me, was given it. It is exquisite, decorated with tiny roses...

Your loving daughter

Genevieve

The historical facts were interesting. Jenny couldn't imagine what it must have been like. She wished she'd known Genevieve. Jenny picked up the next letter.

18 Septembre 1917

Ma chère mère et mon père

I am sorry it has been so long since I wrote to you. I hope you are not too worried. We are now in Kiev, where the Dowager Empress has been persuaded by her family to travel to Crimea with other family members, so we will be on the move again. We have travelled so much over the last few years, I think it is time that the possessions of Her Imperial Highness knew how to pack themselves...

...I expect you heard that Czar Nicholas abdicated in March. The Dowager Empress travelled from Kiev to meet him in Mogilev. She was there for the day...

...I do not know when I will be able to write again, the fighting is

getting very intense.

Your ever-loving daughter

Genevieve

6 Juillet 1918

Ma chère mère et mon père

We have received the news that the Czar and his entire family have been murdered. This is so shocking, we cannot believe it. Her Imperial Highness does not believe it and says it is just a rumour. Her Diary was open on her desk this morning, and I happened to read that she believes her son and his family have escaped out of Russia and that the Bolsheviks are trying to hide the truth...

... The Dowager Empress still refuses to leave Russia...

Genevieve

25 Mars 1919

Ma chère mère et mon père

We have left Russia, the Dowager Queen Alexandra of Great Britain has persuaded Her Imperial Highness to leave. We are currently in Malta before sailing to London…

…Etienne has asked me to marry him, he has asked Madame for permission, which she has granted, which means I will be leaving her service. She asked him what his plans were, and he told her he wanted to return to farming. Her Imperial Highness has given us money to purchase a farm and land as a wedding gift. It is somewhere in the middle of England…

…my personal effects have been packed and sent home to you so do not be surprised when they turn up. Once I have settled Madame in London with her sister, I shall be coming home to see you before returning to a new life in England with Etienne. I am so looking forward to seeing you all again. I'm sure Cecile must have changed a lot since I last saw you all.

I look forward to being home soon

Your loving daughter

Genevieve

Jenny felt like she had just experienced part of history,

reading it first hand from her great, great, grandmothers letters. Her great, great, grandfather had also been in service, how romantic, and how lucky they were to have worked for the Russian Royal family. Having studied Russian History as part of her degree, Jenny knew that these letters were authentic, but it still felt strange to read about it from someone who was there and had experienced it all. She wondered what other gifts had been given. There had been no sign of the hair comb. Opening the small black box and unwrapping the chatelaine, it was now obvious that this had belonged to Genevieve, presumably in her capacity as a personal maid to the Dowager Empress.

Over the next couple of days, Jenny related to her colleagues at work, that she had received a couple of books in the post, but didn't know who they had come from. None of them could shed any light on the puzzle. It was very mystifying to receive items as gifts and not know who they had come from. Later, on Thursday evening, Jenny received a message from Meredith, one of her chums on line friends.

Hi Jenny, hope you had a great Christmas! Sorry I haven't been in touch recently, but Pierre whisked me away on a fabulous skiing holiday, just got back.

Jenny told her about the mysterious gifts and remembered the two Christmas cards with their rows of numbers.

Perhaps they're connected. Maybe the sender of the cards has sent you a clue as to decrypt them.

Why hadn't she considered that, thought Jenny, and after chatting about work, they both said goodbye. Meredith and Jenny had been friends for approximately three years, they had never met, but had formed a good friendship. It was a joy of literature that had brought them together, both having joined an online literature forum. Throughout the last year, Meredith had been the one person, apart from her parents, that Jenny had poured her heart out to. Meredith was able to give comfort having experienced something similar herself, though she said her husband had been found shacked up with someone else a few hundred miles away.

Jenny wandered through to the kitchen and rifled through the pile of Christmas cards she had received. She hadn't bothered to put any of them up, or any decorations, she couldn't face Christmas in the house on her own, and they sat in a scattered pile on the kitchen table. They weren't hard to find with all the glitter on them and she took them back to the living room along with the two books. She examined each card to see if she had missed anything, but could see nothing new. How could a book of sonnets and a cryptic crossword book tell her anything about the cards?

CHAPTER EIGHT

One of the cards was lying face down and it suddenly dawned on her that 'from the mixed group of nonets – printed in Great Britain' was something she would expect to see as a cryptic clue. Mixed group of nonets. Nonet was a description for a group of nine. There were eighteen figures in *26.3 71.123 71.526 ~~not~~ 97.123*, could that be two lots of nine? There were nine figures in *10+6+5+5+22+11=V*, no that didn't make sense. Of course, nonets was an anagram of sonnet, ker-ching, now she was getting somewhere. The little grey cells were starting to kick into gear, and she realised that *10+6+5+5+22+11=V* was possibly a code for sonnet. Jenny looked at the alphabet and the corresponding letter to the number given, *J+F+E+E+T+K=V*, that didn't make sense. Next, she added 9 to each number in turn *19+15+14+14+5+20=V,* and applied the letter to the number of the alphabet, *S+O+N+N+E+T=V*. Jenny puzzled over what was V, could it be verses, voice, roman numeral? She added nine to V and got *XIV = 14* of course, 14 lines in a sonnet. It hadn't taken that long to sort that out had it? She decided that she needed a drink before starting on the row of numbers and helped herself to a single malt that had been Michaels.

Taking the first number 26.3 Jenny turned to page 26 of the book of sonnets, a blank page. Next, she turned to sonnet 26, of which the third word was 'my'. Not sure if this was correct, she turned to line 3. It read:

To thee I send this written ambassage.

'What the heck is an ambassage?'

The notes at the back of the book indicated that it was a variant of embassage, which meant a message. She looked at the next number, 71.123 – there were only fourteen lines in a sonnet. Was it the one hundred and twenty-third word? She quickly counted the words, it was the last word 'gone'. If 26.3 meant *my* and the second word was *gone*… no that didn't make sense at all. In her haste, Jenny hadn't read any of the words, and looking back at the poem, she realised that the numbers should read 71.1 to 3

No longer mourn for me when I am dead

Then you shall hear the surly sullen bell

Give warning to the world that I am fled

Jenny looked at the words in bewilderment – someone was playing a game, surely. Her heart felt like it was made of lead, each heartbeat felt like a tolling bell. She took a mouthful of whisky, then drained the glass and refilled it. She looked at the next number. 71.5 to 6 ~~not~~

Nay, if you read this line, remember not

The hand that writ it; for I love you so

If she removed the word 'not'… Jenny shrieked, it couldn't be, could it? She threw the book down on the coffee table as if it had burnt her hand. Blinking away a tear, she picked the book up and turned to the last number 97.1 to 3

How like a winter hath my absence been

From thee, the pleasure of the fleeting year!

What freezings have I felt, what dark days seen!

She sat staring at the verses, feeling shocked. Her heart beat had quickened as she wrote the lines down on a notepad to read as a single message. Could she dare hope that it was possible that Michael wasn't dead, and had sent her a message. He loved her and missed her. But, if he was alive, where was he? What if it wasn't Michael? Could anybody be spiteful enough to taunt her like this. Jenny felt just as bewildered as before. Her emotions ran through confusion, hope, shock and anger. She decided to try and believe that Michael was out there somewhere and was trying to get a message to her. She lost count of the number of times she re-read the lines. Having fallen asleep where she sat, she opened her eyes and moved stiffly. It was after 2am and the central heating had turned off three hours ago. She read the lines once more.

Jenny's mother rang, as promised at the weekend. Jenny didn't tell her about the cryptic Christmas cards and the messages, she still wasn't totally convinced herself. She wasn't really concentrating on the phone call, but she seemed to be giving the right answers to questions her mother asked her.

'So don't forget to keep an eye on the house while we're away' said her mother, which brought Jenny back to focus on what was being said, 'You've got your keys, and I'll leave the fridge stocked up for you.'

Jenny had forgotten that she was going to house-sit in a week's time while her parents were abroad. 'Catching some rays', was how her father had described it. Jenny had some time owing to her and had turned down the invitation to go with them, but had offered to house-sit instead. Looking at a different set of four walls would be just as good as a holiday away and she would be able to investigate the attic for any other family items.

Having ended the conversation, Jenny picked up the post that had just plopped onto the mat. It was mostly leaflets for furniture, double-glazing and life insurance, but one envelope caught her eye. It had no stamp. She tore it open and found a postcard of Birmingham. On the back of it were a row of numbers *136.13   50.122   75.122   109.526   I (WILL)*. Jenny ran through to the living room and opened up the book of sonnets immediately, writing down each of the lines.

Make but my name thy love, and love that still,

How heavy do I journey on the way,

When what I seek, my weary travel's end,

So are you to my thoughts as food to life,

Or as sweet-season'd showers are to the ground;

That is my home of love: if I have rang'd,

Like him that travels I (will) return again.

The more she thought about it, Jenny knew that this was typical of Michael to send her a message in some sort of puzzle and the postcard of Birmingham seemed almost to confirm it. He had proposed to her through a game of scrabble. He had a secret stash of tiles which he had managed to swop each time he had picked up new ones from the pile, managing to put out the words 'will you marry me'. Her heart felt lighter, but her head spun with questions. Where was he, where had he been, why, when would he be home?

CHAPTER NINE

Monday morning at work, a man approached the desk to ask if there were any books on villages in the United Kingdom. He was of medium height with dark brown hair. He didn't maintain eye contact, which Jenny took as him being shy.

'Are there any particular villages that you are interested in?'

'M-m-middle England, I g-g-guess.'

She showed him the aisle where he could browse a number of books and returned to her desk. She had no sooner settled herself at her computer when another man approached. He had dark hair, from what she could see under the large fedora style hat and was wearing a sports jacket with chinos and loafers without socks. Over his shoulder, he wore a satchel style bag.

'There's a style icon, not.' Jenny thought to herself.

'Excuse me, could you help me please? I'm looking for books on well-dressing. Could you point me in the right direction?'

'Yes of course, if you'd like to follow me.'

He looked vaguely familiar, even though he was wearing large sunglasses, favoured by the rich and famous.

'I hope you don't mind me asking, but, do I know you?'

'No, I don't think so, but you may have seen me on the television some time. I'm a part-time actor, Simon Pellham.'

He held out his hand and as Jenny went to shake it, he grasped it gently and kissed the back of it.

'Ah, that would be it.' Though she couldn't think of any programmes that he might have been in. 'Here you are, I hope you find the book you're looking for.'

A few minutes later the man returned to the desk having decided on a book he would like to borrow. The front cover showed a village that Jenny knew well, it was Wartlington. 'I grew up in that village' volunteered Jenny, 'the well-dressing festival is well worth a visit in the area.'

'That is a wonderful thing. I'll make sure I visit it sometime. How do I check this out?'

'If you take the book over to the machine by the door you can scan your library card and then the back of any books you wish to borrow.'

'Thank you for your help. Have a good day.'

Jenny found the book an hour later sitting on the trolley that returned books were put, waiting to be put away. Puzzled, she returned the book to its shelf and carried on with her work.

The week flew by and Jenny arrived at the bus stop on Friday afternoon ready for her holiday. As she stood waiting, she could see a drunk weaving his way up the road towards the bus stop. He was wearing a very shabby raincoat that was held together with the belt, the buttons that were left, were hanging by a thread. He wore jogging bottoms, that had clearly seen better days and a football bobble hat that seemed to merge into his shaggy beard. He had clearly had a few drinks too many, bumping into the side of a building, and narrowly missing falling off the kerb. He stopped at the front of the queue and asked where the next bus was going. The remaining people in the queue, all suddenly looked very busy, checking watches and time-tables. The drunk continued to work his way up the queue of people asking different questions, apparently indifferent to whether they wanted to engage with him or not. When he got to Jenny, he stopped and looked at her.

'My you're a bonny wee lass. Ye remind me of my dear old mammy.'

Jenny tried hard not to take a step backwards, she didn't want to show that she was intimidated or scared in any way by this person who was invading her space. He fell into her, wreaking of beer.

'Ooops, sorry. How clumsy.' He apologised profusely and continued his journey up the road. She couldn't help wrinkling up her nose and hoping that the smell wouldn't linger. She put her hand into her pocket to retrieve a tissue and found a piece of paper that was giving off an aroma of beer. Jenny crinkled her nose as the smell wafted upwards, and noticed a message in tiny writing *Take everything with you to your parents. Talk to no-one.* Not wanting to draw attention to herself, she put it back in her pocket underneath her keys, till she got home and could find a magnifying glass. The drunk must have put it in her pocked when he fell against her. When the bus arrived, Jenny got on and paid her fare, looking around her hoping that the smell from the drunk wasn't fixed on her clothing. She looked out of the window to see how far the drunk had progressed, but there was no sign of him. Arriving home, Jenny picked up her post, a bank statement, and walked into the kitchen. She was sure there was a magnifying glass somewhere. She slipped off her coat and put it on the back of one of the kitchen chairs and started searching through the kitchen drawers but found nothing. The bureau in the living room had numerous drawers where she found a magnifying glass. Jenny retrieved the piece of paper from her coat pocket and returned to the bureau. The writing was miniscule, worse than the bottom line at the opticians. Under the magnifying glass, she was able to read

Take everything with you to your parents. Talk to no-one.

'Oh my goodness' exclaimed Jenny her heart suddenly beating fast, 'was that Michael? Eewww disgusting.'

She then wondered why he hadn't said anything to her, but she realised that if he had spoken to her properly, she would have made some sort of a scene.

Jenny packed everything she needed for the week along with her own wren salt and the box she'd brought back with her, at Christmas. With everything safely stowed in her car, she locked the car and took a last walk round her home ensuring that all doors and windows were locked. As a precaution, she placed a small piece of paper in the door-frame of each internal door, so that should anybody enter while she was away, she would know it.

It took Jenny just over an hour to get to Wartlington, which given the fact it was Saturday traffic, wasn't bad. The M6 had been relatively light on traffic and the Toll Road virtually empty. She had remembered to bring the house keys with her, but knew that if she had forgotten them, there was a spare key hidden in one of the garden gnomes in the back garden. She had remonstrated with her parents for leaving a key hidden like that, but they argued back that nobody would look for a house key in a group of gnomes quietly fishing in the back-garden pond, which, they pointed out, was a few hundred metres away from the front door. She opened the front door.

Having deposited her bags inside, Jenny found the garage key hanging up by the telephone, and put her car away. She wasn't planning to use it during the coming week, so it may as well go away. As she got into the car, she thought she saw someone behind the hedge, but as she reversed the car off the drive and round to the garage, there was nobody there. With the car safely in the garage she returned to the house, but there was still that feeling that she was being watched. Once inside, Jenny took her things upstairs to her room and emptied her bags. She looked outside her window and saw the vicar talking to one of the villagers.

She took the black box and the family tree paper back downstairs, lit the fire and made some lunch. Her mother had left some smoked salmon and cream cheese in the fridge with a note that said

Eat me first.

Looking in the bread bin, Jenny found a bagel which she cut in half and smothered with cheese, the salmon and a sprinkling of ground black pepper. The fridge also contained a small bottle of prosecco with yet another note which read

the perfect drink to go with your bagel.

The fire was burning well, so Jenny added a couple of logs and a little more coal to keep it going for a while and sat back down in her chair to look at the letters her great, great, grandmother had written all those years ago. She was half-way through the bundle of letters when there was a knock on the front door. Jenny peered through the net curtains to see if she knew who it was, but the person had their back to her. Nothing for it, she'd have to go and answer it. As she opened the door, Jenny stared in amazement at the figure of the drunk from the bus stop.

'Er, hello' said Jenny 'Can I help you?'

Without saying a word, the drunk pushed past Jenny and shut the door. Jenny gasped when she heard a voice she knew.

'Jen, it's me, I'm sorry for pushing past you, but I'm not sure if I was followed and I didn't want to loiter on the step, just in case.'

Jenny felt as if she was in a dream world and let herself be led into the living room.

'How...? What...? Michael...?'

He took off his bobble hat off and peeled away the beard from his face.

'Jenny I am so sorry to have gone like that...'

She stood staring at him, trying to make sense of what was happening, then she lunged at him and pounded his chest with both hands, pushing him backwards.

'You bastard, you complete and utter bastard. You

obnoxious, self-righteous prick. You disappear without a by your leave, leaving my life in shreds and think you can just waltz back in when you feel like it. Do you have any idea, any idea at all?'

Her shouting changed to sobbing, 'How could you do that? Why couldn't you tell me? Does our marriage mean nothing that you can't talk to me? I mean, where have you been? Why did you go?'

Michael caught hold of her hands and held her in his arms while she sobbed the year away.

Jenny pushed him away fighting her way out of his embrace.

'You smell disgusting.'

He tried to take her back in his arms.

'Don't touch me. I don't know who you are any more. The Michael I know never, ever, failed to let me know if he wasn't coming home yet you, seem to think it's fine to go away without a word then just come back.'

'Jen, I can understand you're cross.'

'CROSS, that doesn't begin to describe what I'm feeling, what I felt or anything.'

'Jen, I'm sorry, what else can I say? I couldn't tell you, as much as I wanted to. If I hadn't gone, your life may well have been in danger, the only way I could protect you was to disappear.' He continued trying to reassure her that he loved her, he was back, and would never go again.

Jenny looked at him in puzzlement. 'How could my life be in danger? You're a personal trainer, or at least that's what you convinced me you were.'

'I was, or at least, that was my cover.'

'COVER'

'Jen stop shouting.'

'NO I BLOODY WELL WILL NOT. What do you mean cover?'

'I work for the Government.'

'Go on, I'm listening. This had better be good.'

'I work undercover for an organisation, something akin to

MI5'.

'You're a spy?'

'I guess that's one description. I work under a different name, one that I'm known by everywhere, except with you and our families.'

Jenny thought the use of families was odd, as he'd told her he was an only child and the only one left in his family. But she let it go without questioning him. She interrupted him.

'Am I allowed to know that name?'

'Yes, it's Simon Pellham, my great grandfather's name on my mother's side.'

'You were in the library... you told me you were an actor called Simon Pellham.'

'The people I work for think it's my real name and that Michael Black is my alias. Any checks they have done on me will show me to be Simon. I told you, I'm going to tell you everything. I had been told by bosses further up the chain of command that I needed to stage my death and that you would have received a healthy pension. But I couldn't do that to you. I knew I'd come back to you. You see, I wasn't supposed to fall in love with you in the first place, which would have made faking my death not such a bad scenario.'

'For you maybe, but what about me? Are there other families in this situation?'

'Sadly yes. It's all part of being undercover, having a second life, and before you ask, no there is no-one else.'

'Where you ever in the army and what about the gym? When I rang them they hadn't heard of you.'

'I was recruited from the army and I used 'Fitness For You' as a customer, under my alias. The work I was doing was in danger of being leaked to the press, so I was pulled out by my boss without any warning. I've spent the last year in Europe, and although the new case hasn't closed yet, the operation has now moved to the UK.'

Jenny sat down on the settee shaking her head in bewilderment staring at Michael as if he was a ghost.

'You are really here, aren't you? I've imagined I've seen you so many times…'

'Yes, love, I'm here.'

'I want to celebrate, let fireworks off, but at the same time, I don't want to, in case I'm dreaming. God, I'm so confused about all this. I mean you disappear, and now just when I feel like I'm getting my life back on track, you turn up again. I don't know what to think.'

When Jenny's tears subsided enough she asked 'are you going to stay dressed like that, or are you going to revert back to yourself?'

'If it's ok with you, I'll go and have a quick shower, get rid of this clothing'.

'Please tell me you're going to dispose of it, it stinks.'

'Have you got a bin bag?'

'Hang on, I'll go and fetch you one.'

Michael went upstairs while Jenny sat in her chair staring at the fire, trying to make sense of what had just happened. Her head pounded and felt like it had exploded. She'd wanted him back so much, now he was here, she wasn't sure how to feel, apart from very confused. She fetched a black bag from the kitchen and took it upstairs and sat down on the edge of her bed. The shower switched off and

Michael appeared in her bedroom, a towel wrapped around his waist, and another over his shoulders. He stood in the doorway looking as handsome as ever and a look on his face that asked the question if he was welcome back. Jenny walked over to him.

'Michael, I have missed you so much, I can't find the words to say how much and...' she stopped as their lips touched and he kissed her, she kissed him back gently at first, then more passionately. Jenny released his towel, by which time he was undressing her. They fell on the bed and discovered each other anew. They lay for some time, legs and arms entwined, happy to be back in each other's company.

Michael spoke first 'come on Mrs Black, let's go and see if we can resurrect that fire downstairs.'

'Am I Mrs Black, Michael?'

'Yes you are 100% legally and totally Mrs Michael Black. Now let's go downstairs and I'll do my best to unravel this conundrum.'

He bent down and pulled a travel bag out from under the bed.

Jenny stared in amazement. 'How… when… how did that get there?'

'I used the spare key from the garden gnome. I managed to get back out of here just before you arrived, then I hid in the garden. The vicar was talking to someone and I didn't want him to see me, I just wanted to see you so I waited till he drove off.'

'I told my parents that leaving a key hidden was dangerous' Jenny laughed 'but so glad they did, I think. Have you put those disgusting clothes in the bin bag?'

'Yes, I'll go and put it in the bin outside.'

Downstairs, the fire was still burning and didn't take much interference to get back to full strength. Jenny disappeared down to her father's den reappearing moments later with a half bottle of champagne.

'I don't think dad will mind this extravagance, given the circumstances' and fetched a couple of champagne flutes from the drinks cabinet.

They settled themselves on the settee and nestled into each other.

'Do you want me to ask questions, or will you just tell me everything?'

'Well, let me start back to before we met. I have to confess that I engineered our meeting.'

Jenny didn't seem that surprised at this revelation.

'I'd seen you a few times at the library and fell instantly in love with you. I didn't want to approach you and get turned down. A wimp, I know.'

'So, come on sunshine, tell me how you got me to meet you in Birmingham?'

'Well it wasn't ultra-difficult. I used the tricks and devices that some mind-readers use, that of auto-suggestion. There was a poster in the library staff-room, I borrowed books which you helped me find on Birmingham, and various titles with blind and date in them. I possibly mentioned all three words in conversation with you a few times, so by the time I dropped the leaflet through your door, or rather I gave it to the postman to put through with your post, you were primed. My friend is the manager of the bar where the event took place, and after a couple of drinks, he agreed that if you turned up, I would be your first date.'

'Incredible. You went to all those lengths just to ask me out. So, if you managed to persuade the postman to put a leaflet through the door, did you do the same with the two Christmas cards and postcard, which I presume you sent?'

'Yes, I've been close to home for a few weeks, there was a serious possibility that you might have seen me. Well, actually you did see me, dressed as a drunk.'

'Yes, twice now. That was disgusting.'

'It was a good disguise though, wasn't it? I had doused my clothing under the coat in beer, wiped it around my face and … well it smelt bad enough to me.'

'Any other disguises I might know about?'

'Well, not so much a disguise, but there was the driver in the red car at the supermarket, just before Christmas. I waited till I saw you reverse out and came round the corner quickly, I needed to see your face, and at least you didn't swear at me' he grinned. 'There was the hippy on the train, I watched you the whole journey through my hair, and I'm afraid I was that objectionable passenger who wouldn't let that poor man, who'd helped you with your luggage, have his seat, and in the library, which you've already sussed. I haven't been far from you, for very long in these last few weeks. In fact, I've spoken to you nearly every week for the whole year.'

Jenny found this statement hard to swallow 'Oh come off it, I know I haven't spoken to you till today, well, apart from unknowingly in the library.'

'Well' Michael grimaced 'I'm Meredith.'

Jenny almost spat out her mouthful of drink. She laughed and then looked at him in stunned amazement and almost dropped her glass. 'What?'

'I'm Meredith. I set it up before we got married, so that should I get pulled out at any time, I could stay in touch with you somehow. We've had some great conversations, haven't we?'

Jenny didn't know what to say, she sat staring at Michael, amazed at his revelation. He'd used all the clichéd words in the conversations that she hated like 'Hun', 'bestie', 'babe' and 'sweetie'.

'But you never showed any interest in Chums Online. You said it was for people who had nothing better to do and that I was wasting my time being on it. I mean, you didn't even know how to set up my privacy on it, when I asked for your help.'

'Um, well, I guess you ought to know that I did set your privacy options on your Chums Online page, and…'

'Out with it' demanded Jenny.

'Well the telephone is bugged…'

'Which is how you knew my travel plans' finished Jenny.

'It was all part of keeping you safe.'

'I still don't understand this about keeping me safe.'

'It's very complicated…'

'What about coming into our home? Did you do that at all?' She demanded.

'Just the once. I was careful not to touch or move anything, I just needed to be there.'

Like a fencing duel, Jenny reposted

'Well sunshine, I have news for you, you did touch and

move something. I thought I was going mad. You picked up the post and put it on the coffee table.'

Michael shook his head 'No, no I didn't, it was already on the table in a neat pile.' They looked at each other. Someone had been in the house, but who?

'Why on earth didn't you just contact me, like any normal person?'

'Because I was being followed. I didn't want to put you in any danger, but equally, I wanted to let you know I was around, hence the coded messages.'

It was starting to get dark. Michael stood up, crossed the room and drew the curtains, then switched on the lamps that were scattered around the room, giving off a soft warm light. He stoked the fire and added another log.

'Is there anything to eat? 'I'm starving.'

Jenny told him that the fridge was full of food and that perhaps they should go and find something. She re-filled their glasses and followed him to the kitchen. Opening the fridge, Jenny noticed that there was enough food for a couple of weeks. At lunch time, she hadn't looked beyond the salmon and cream cheese. There were two steaks on a plate covered in plastic food film with one of her mother's messages,

For Saturday evening, enjoy your meal and your friend's company.

'How did mum know I was having company?'

'Um, I might have sent her an email from you saying I hope she didn't mind, but I had invited a friend to stay the weekend who would be arriving in time for an evening meal.'

'So, you had access to my email account as well?' Jenny looked at Michael in disbelief.

'Er, yes, that's how I was able to delete all traces of emails.'

'Unbelievable, at least you have the good grace to stand there looking sheepish. I think the least you can do is cook these steaks. I'll go and fetch your glass from the living room.'

Jenny returned to the kitchen with Michael's glass and the bottle.

'There is some peppercorn sauce in the fridge, do you want

any?

Jenny sat shaking her head. 'You are an enigma Mr Black, one moment I think I know you completely, then the next moment I wonder if I know you at all and yes please for the sauce. Do you actually do anything that is straight-forward?'

'Probably not.'

'What else are you cooking?'

'Well your wonderful mother has provided some new potatoes, stemmed broccoli and mange-tout, and I've found a dessert, tart au citron. Boy does your mum know how to stock a fridge. Five more minutes and it should all be ready.'

Jenny sat staring at the back of Michael as he finished cooking the meal. He'd been gone from her life for a year. Did he have no idea what she'd been through, what she'd felt like? And now, just as she was starting to get used to life on her own, he walked back into it. She stood up and fetched a couple of plates from the kitchen cupboard and knives and forks. She refilled their glasses and emptied the bottle.

'Do you think your dad would mind if we had another

bottle?' Michael asked.

Without waiting to answer, Jenny dashed down stairs to relieve her father of another bottle of champagne. She decided that she would replenish the stocks before her parents returned home.

The steaks were cooked to perfection, just slightly pink in the middle. The whole meal was delicious and having washed up, they settled back on the sofa in front of the fire.

'Where have you been working during the year?'

'I've been in a few different European countries, Russia, France, Germany, Ukraine, Croatia, Greece, Denmark and Malta, to name just a few and now the UK. There is a dissident group in Russia and the UK who are hunting missing items from the Romanov family. The most valuable items appear to be the Easter Eggs made by Faberge between 1855 and 1916. Emperor Alexander III gave his wife Empress Maria Feodorovna an egg to celebrate the twentieth anniversary of their engagement and from then on, he gave her an egg each year until his death, when their son Tsar Nicholas II carried on the tradition, giving both his wife and his mother an egg. The eggs were very ornate and contained at least one surprise inside such as a miniature replica of the Coronation Coach, pendants, photographs and animals. When the Tsar and his family were murdered, it was not known what had become of their personal effects. Most of the eggs are in private collections around the world, but there are perhaps seven, maybe more, that are missing. It wasn't until the Kremlin archives were opened in the 1990s that people were able to see some of these eggs. Many of the pre-revolutionary pieces have a stock number engraved on them which, now that records have been discovered, can be checked to see if they are authentic. Unfortunately, at least three of the eggs at the Kremlin have been found to not have a number, which the records show, they should have. It is thought that they are fakes and that the originals are missing. Since 1998, two have been found in private collections, but a third is still missing. It is the Hen with Sapphire Pendant, also known as The Egg with Hen in Basket, made in 1886 for Alexander III who presented it to his wife.'

Jenny sat enraptured by what she was hearing. She remembered the newspaper article she had found under the fridge, but didn't mention it. 'Did that have anything to do with Michael's disappearing act', she wondered?

'Faberge was publicly denounced as a 'profiteer' and has

since been accused by this dissident group of making copies. Whether this is true or not, nobody knows, but it is highly unlikely. Russia wants its jewels back, and have hired the group, who seem intent on recovering all lost items for a handsome pay-out. After the fall of the Romanov dynasty, the royal art collections were raided and the eggs were taken to Moscow and remained hidden there in the Kremlin. The Dowager Empress is known to have fled with one egg, which is in Denmark, but the question is, did she take any others with her?' So, I have been following the group around Europe, gathering my own intelligence. It would appear that they have been retracing journeys made by the Romanov's and the Dowager Empress.'

Michael looked at Jenny, she'd fallen asleep. 'Too much champagne, huh, you can't hack it.' He woke her gently and suggested they turn in for the night.

Jenny agreed and found her way to the stairs, 'don't be long, I'll be waiting' she smiled.

'I'll be up immediately I've checked the doors are locked and made the fire safe.

Michael took his mobile out of his pocket and checked for messages, then took the glasses to the kitchen and ensured the door was locked. He switched off the light, closed the door and put a fire-guard in front of the dying embers. He made his way to the stairs and checked that the front door was also locked. Switching off the downstairs lights, he made his way to the bedroom and started to undress.

'I'm here, love...'

He was interrupted with gentle snoring coming from the bed before he could say anything more, so removed the rest of his clothing, switched off the light and stole a look through the curtains before climbing in beside her.

Jenny awoke the next morning, not with a headache, but a heavy feeling as if her brain had been overloaded with mush. She looked over at the other side of the bed, and noticed it had been slept in. In wasn't a dream then, he really was here. On cue, Michael came in through the bedroom door with a large tray.

'Hello sleepyhead, I've brought us breakfast in bed. There were some croissants in the freezer, so they are fresh out of the oven. There is scrambled egg, bacon, orange juice and freshly brewed coffee. So, sit up, get yourself comfortable and we'll begin'.

He smiled at her with that boyish grin that made her go all gooey inside.

'Did you sleep well?' he asked. 'At one point, I thought the London express was coming through the village, but when I stroked your thigh, you murmured thank-you and turned over.'

'I do not snore' Jenny argued 'unless I'm congested or...'

'Drunk too much champagne' Michael interjected.

Jenny giggled. 'Sorry, it must have been all the excitement of yesterday, there is only so much a girl can handle all at once.' With that she pushed the tray out of the way and pulled Michael over so he landed on top of her 'and I think I need to handle this right now.'

They kissed slowly and tenderly, their hands exploring each other's body as if creating a map in their imaginations of what the other looked and felt like. In their passion, the tray fell to the floor with a bang, but it didn't disturb their love-making. They nestled into each other's arms and lay dozing until the church bell started chiming, calling people to church for the 11am service.

Jenny got up first and ran a shower. She came back into the bedroom where she found Michael looking at his mobile. 'Everything OK?' she asked.

'Err, yes, yes, everything's fine. Someone has tried ringing you at home, three times in the last few minutes. They haven't left a message, which is strange, if they can't get hold of you, and they've rung three times, there must be something they want to say.'

'Do you know the number that called?

'No, number withheld. I'll go and have a shower now. I think you might need to clean the carpet, there's a coffee stain!'

Jenny threw her wet towel at him, which he deftly caught as he quickly escaped to the bathroom.

Half an hour later, Jenny had cleared up the mess in the bedroom, sponged the coffee splot on the carpet, raked out the ashes from yesterday's fire and lit a new one. She beamed at Michael as he came downstairs, nothing could describe how she felt having him back. 'Would you like another coffee?' she asked.

'Yes please, in fact, I'll make it, I'll be back in a jiffy'.

'The kettle's boiled' Jenny called after him.

Michael was back a few minutes later with two mugs of steaming coffee. 'How much of what I was telling you last night, do you remember?

'Um, well… did I fall asleep?'

'Yep'

'Well I remember you saying that the Dowager Empress had left Russia with at least one egg. If you said much after that, then no I don't remember.

'Ah well, in that case, you missed the bit where I said I'd followed the group on their jaunt around Europe following in the Romanov footsteps.'

'Michael'

'Yes love'

'I think my great, great, grandparents were in service to the Dowager Empress.'

'What makes you think that?'

Do you remember that letter I found a couple of years ago?'

'Vaguely.'

'Well, there's a trunk in the cellar and I found all sorts of things in it that must have belonged to my great, great, grandmother and the letters that her parents talked about in the letter where there.'

'Have you got the letters with you? It would be great to have a look at them'.

'They're here, I was looking at them yesterday when you arrived. Most of them are illegible, but some of them are ok. One or two have a page missing or water marks, but here you are.'

Jenny handed the bundle of letters over to Michael who read what he could.

'These are amazing. I would agree with you that your great, great, grandparents were indeed working for the family. What else did you say was in the trunk?'

Jenny picked up the black box that was sitting on the floor beside her chair. She opened the smaller black box and retrieved the chatelaine in its tissue paper wrapping and handed it to Michael. He inspected each chain and item and concurred that they were gold.

'What a wonderful item to have. Genevieve must have been given this, she would never have been able to afford it. Presumably the Dowager gave it to her, she seems to have been generous with other gifts, according to these letters.'

Jenny showed him the four books. 'Must be where I get my love of literature from' she said, as she picked up the wren. There was also this. She held out the tissue wrapped object. Michael unwrapped it carefully and looked at her in puzzlement.

'It's an exact copy of the one I have.' Jenny delved into her bag and brought out the wren she'd had all her life. 'The top should lift off, but it seems wedged on, and I didn't want to apply too much force, in case I damaged it.'

'I think I might be able to get this off.' Michael went out to the kitchen. Jenny followed. 'Do you have a cotton-bud?'

'Yes, there are some in the bathroom, hang on, I'll go and get one.' Jenny ran up the stairs and arrived back with said cotton-bud in hand. Michael had put on her mother's washing up gloves and taking the cotton-bud off Jenny, applied a little washing up liquid to the end and gently stroked it around the join on the wren. After a minute, he gently twisted the two halves.

'I think it's working, I'll give it another going round with the cotton-bud'. He waited another minute and gently twisted the two halves again. Success. He peeled off the gloves and grabbed a piece of kitchen paper to wipe any excess of liquid off. Sitting in the ceramic bowl was a folded-up piece of tissue paper. Michael set the lump of tissue paper down on the kitchen table and carefully opened the layers. There was a lot of paper for what was lying within.

'A key! I wonder what it's for and why hidden away?'

Michael put the wren back together and examined the key. Let's go and have a look at the trunk downstairs, I have an idea what this might be for.

CHAPTER TEN

Jenny led the way down to the cellar. Michael was impressed with the sensor lighting and even more impressed with what his father-in-law had done down there. Amazed, he inspected the bottles of drink available. There were at least eight bottles of single malt, all different, and as many different gins, vodka, rum, brandy, sherry, port and cordials

'Bloody hell, Jen, he'll put the pub out of business with this lot. I think I'll retire and live in the cellar' he laughed.

'Help yourself to a drink, and while you're at it, I'll have a gin and tonic please. There's a fridge under the bar with tonic and ice'

Michael chose a whisky he'd never tried before and locating the fridge took out a tin of tonic and a couple of ice-cubes. 'Do you want sugar-free tonic or full-blown sugary one?

'Sugar-free please.'

The trunk was still sitting away from the wall and Jenny opened it so that Michael could see inside it. Handing Jenny her drink, he placed his own on the coffee table before removing the bags of clothing from the trunk. At the bottom, he found what he was looking for and called Jenny over.

'Look, can you see those ridges on the bottom and at the side?

'Where… Oh yes, I didn't notice those before. What are they for?

'Well, taking an educated guess, I would say there was some sort of lockable case in there, which that key we have just found in the salt, would open. Those ridges would have held the case in place. However, as you can see from the now empty trunk, there is no such case here.'

'Mum did say she thought there were some more items in the attic, I wonder if that's where it is?'

They sat down on the chairs and Jenny showed Michael some of the clothing she'd uncovered as they finished their drinks.

'Right' said Michael, 'let's put these things back away in the trunk and go and investigate the attic.'

They washed up their glasses and went up the cellar stairs.

In the living room, Jenny put another log on the fire and some more coal, and ensuring the fire-guard was in place, they carried on upstairs to the attic. There was no hatch in the ceiling like Jenny had in her house. Her father had built an enclosed staircase so that Jenny's mother could access her workroom easily, which was walled off from the rest of the attic. Michael and Jenny looked around for anything that might look like a box that had been removed from the trunk. It was very dusty and not very warm.

'I don't think anyone's been up here in a long while and certainly not since mum had her craft room made.'

Jenny found her way to the far corner of the space, climbing over boxes of clothes, toys and her rocking horse. What she didn't expect to find was a rotavator and a lawn mower. She shook her head in disbelief and walked straight into a cobweb which made her scream. It wasn't that she disliked spiders, it was the fact that this web was so big it covered her face. Michael laughed and called her a wuss, but he looked in amazement as he saw behind her was the very box they were searching for.

'Look, behind you, that looks about the right size and shape off the box that should be in the trunk.'

'Where, I can't see anything.'

'Against the wall. Put your hand out… left a bit more. That's it.'

There was a good layer of dust on it, making it hard to discern what its colour was. Michael made his way over to Jenny, stepping over the rocking horse as if it were the most natural thing in the world to do.

'That's it, that's the case that would have been in the trunk. Let's get it out of here and get it downstairs where it will be warmer, and there'll be more light'. He lifted the box causing a plume of dust to rise up into his face, which in turn made him sneeze and his eyes water.

'Now who's the wuss' laughed Jenny as she took the box off him so that he could navigate around the toys and boxes.

Back downstairs, Jenny found an old cloth which she held under a tap for a couple of minutes before wringing it out.

'Here, wipe the box with this, it should get rid of most of the dust.'

As Michael wiped the box, the most beautiful crimson

leather gleamed at the world.

'Another gift from the Dowager, do you think?' asked Michael.

'It must be, it's gorgeous, it must have cost a huge amount of money, Genevieve would surely never have been able to afford this.'

Jenny stroked the leather, it was so soft. She picked the key up off the sideboard, where they had left it when they went upstairs to the attic. Inserting it into the lock, it turned easily as if it had only been used yesterday. They tentatively opened the door. Inside was another door and two drawers underneath it, each of them covered in the same crimson leather and all of them locked. Michael tried the key in the door lock but it wouldn't open. He took the key out and examined the lock. As far as he could see, the key should work.

'I've got a set of skeleton keys upstairs, I'll go and fetch them to see if they'll work.'

Jenny stared after him in amazement. Skeleton keys, presumably part of the kit used by spies she thought.

Jenny picked up the box, sat it on her lap and tried the key in the drawer locks. As she pushed the key in and turned it, she applied a little pressure and the drawer sprang open. She tried the second drawer which also sprang open. By the time Michael reappeared with his set of skeleton keys, Jenny had applied the same principle to the door.

'Eureka' she cried, 'how clever is that?'

Michael picked up the box and placed it on the coffee table and they looked inside the cupboard of the box. It was lined in a luxurious dark blue velvet.

'This must have held something very precious' whispered Jenny, 'the sides are slightly padded as if to protect its bounty.'

'Why are you whispering' laughed Michael.

'I don't know, it just seems so… so imperial.'

'Well I think you've hit that one on the head, I can only imagine that this belonged to the Empress at some stage in her life. Do you think Genevieve took it when she left as a memento?

Jenny looked at him in amazement, hurt that he thought

one of her relatives would pinch something.

'Why would she take it, when she'd been given so many other things, that doesn't make sense. No I think she was given this, yet another gift from the Dowager Empress. I wonder what was in it originally.'

'Maybe it's the case for one of those Faberge eggs. Perhaps something that is in there now, will give us a clue.' Michael replied, reaching for his mobile that was buzzing in his pocket. He looked at the screen and Jenny could see a look of anger covering his face.

'Jen, I know I've just got back, and I wouldn't say this if it wasn't necessary, but I need to go out for a few hours, I promise I'll be back either late this evening or in the morning, but I'll let you know which.'

Jenny glared at him. She'd only just got him back, and he was going again. Tears filled her eyes, which she tried to blink away.

'I can't believe that you've walked back into my life, and now you're going again. I was right, you really are a complete and utter bastard. Is it urgent? Do you really have to go? Can't it wait?'

Feelings of shock and anger filled her. How could he even think of going out and leaving her. He had no empathy whatsoever.

'Yes love, it is urgent and it's to do with work. The house may have been broken into and I need to go and check everything is ok. The phone has been tampered with and it's sending me an alert message.'

'I'll come with you' she said, standing up not wanting to let him out of her sight.

'No, please stay here. It will be safer for you. Answer the door to no-one, not even the vicar or any of the neighbours. You have everything you need here, so there is no need to go out.' Michael sounded very insistent which Jenny took as an order. 'Perhaps I shouldn't have come back yet. Perhaps it was too soon.'

'I just don't understand…' She began to cry.

'Come on, dry your eyes, I will be back, I promise. Look, here's my mobile number, if you need me urgently'. He handed her card with a number scribbled on it. 'It's only a temporary number, so don't put it in your address book.'

Jenny picked her car keys up and gave them to Michael 'you'll need these then.'

'No' Michael replied, I have a car, it's in the pub car park, the landlord said I could leave it there while I visited my relatives in the village, as they didn't have any spare car park space.' He went upstairs and came back down wearing a jumper, jacket and a scarf round his neck that covered his mouth, and a peaked cap. Jenny pulled the scarf down, kissed him, and told him to stay safe. As she hugged him, she could feel a slight bulge on his right hip and she looked at him questioningly.

'It's protection.' Michael said firmly 'Just remember I love you and I will be back. Is there anything I should look to see might be missing?'

'The only thing of value to me is our wedding photos. I have all my jewellery and all the items from Christmas, and the trunk here. I really wish you weren't going. Be safe.'

He kissed her one last time and was gone. Jenny stared out of the window as he went down the garden path, then ran upstairs to her parent's bedroom to see him leave from the pub car park. She was having difficulty making sense of how she was feeling. Part of her wanted to tell him to not come back, but he'd reawakened her feelings for him. As she looked out of the bedroom window she saw him climb into a red fiesta, the one from the supermarket car park, she thought. Jenny waved at the car as he left, even though she knew he couldn't see her, and with a sigh, she returned downstairs and attended to the fire. She wasn't sure how she was supposed to feel, but she knew this was odd behaviour. Michael had just come back and now he was gone again. It didn't make sense at all.

Jenny picked up her mobile and dialled the number that Michael had left.

'Hello, are you ok? I've only just got in the car.'

'I know, I saw you from the upstairs window. I just wanted to check that the number worked.'

'Why wouldn't it?'

'I can't believe you have to ask me that when a year ago your mobile suddenly stopped working.' Jenny replied crossly.

'Sorry love, I should have thought.'

'Yes you bloody well should have.'

'I'm sorry. I'll be back as quickly as I can.'

'Ok… bye.'

Jenny tried to take her mind off Michael's unexpected departure by looking inside the box, where she found an assortment of papers amongst which was an envelope, addressed to her grandfather, which contained a letter from Genevieve. Before reading it, Jenny got herself a coffee and a sandwich, stoked the fire and got herself comfortable.

CHAPTER ELEVEN

14 October 1960

My dear grandson, Albert, who brings me such joy in my old age. You asked about what my life was like before I married your grandfather. As you are now about to embark on married life yourself I thought it time to write this down for you.

Etienne and I returned from France in 1921 to our new home in England after visiting my parents. We were married in London in 1920 with the Dowager Empress in attendance. She was so kind to us. She was the most wonderful lady to work for, we served her, and yet she often went out to help with the Russian Red Cross to look after soldiers and others who got injured. She often gave me a little gift to thank me for my patience with her such as a hair comb, odd bits of jewellery, and other trinkets. My job was her personal maid which had me doing everything for Madame, from getting her clothes ready, sorting out her laundry, doing her hair, getting the jewels she wanted to wear from the great safe, and organising her things when she travelled. Etienne was her chauffeur. She ruled her family, which people complained at and mocked her, but she did what any loving mother did, cared for her children and wanted only the best for them. I had to agree with Madame when that man Rasputin was brought in by the Czarina. He was very odd. He would walk around the palace running

*his beads through his hand, stroking his beard and treating the rest of
us staff as if we were beneath him. He was a bit odd or eccentric.
Madame considered him to have far too much influence over the
Imperial family and asked on many occasions for him to be dismissed.
The Czar always left it to the Czarina to comment, he didn't want to
upset either his wife or his mother. The situation was sort of resolved
when Rasputin's body was found in a river, there is still a mystery as
to how he died.*

*Etienne and I travelled everywhere with Madame, and came to
England a few times, as well as her trips back to Denmark. For such
an independent woman, she seemed to rely on us very much. We were
sad to leave her, but it was not done for married women to remain in
service, such as this. When we reached Malta, having left Russia for
ever, Etienne asked Madame for permission to marry. She insisted
that she buy us a home, and we purchased this farm with the money
she gave us. Etienne's dream came true owning and running his own
business.*

*My parents, your great grandparents, lived in France, but they were
getting old and had no sons to take on their farm, so they sold it and
came here to live with us. I was expecting a baby, your father, so
having my mother here was a huge relief.*

My sister, Cecile, met a young gentleman, Mark Carruthers, on the boat when she was coming over to visit us, from France, when we were still in London with Madame. They seem to have fallen instantly in love! We didn't see much of her during her visit, she spent most of it at the young man's family estate. It appears that after the last time we saw her, they were married and he travelled with her to our parents' home. My mother was quite shocked that both her daughters had married within a few weeks of each other and without her in attendance. I think Mark and his family expected a dowry when he married Cecile, but he didn't get one. My parents were not wealthy and the sale of their farm didn't raise much money. I am sure that Cecile thought she had married a very rich gentleman, but sadly, his family were not able to pay for the upkeep of their home or their staff and had to leave the estate. Over the years, Cecile has constantly asked me to help her and Mark out, but all the cash we had went into the farm to pay for our own workers. I have to say, that on the few occasions I met Mark, I did not like him very much. Whether it was his standing in society or his upbringing, I don't know, but he always gave the impression that life owed him something.

While we were only blessed with one child, Cecile and Mark managed to produce seven offspring, before Mark died leaving Cecile to bring up their brood on her own. I did send her the odd pound, when I could, but I doubt it made much difference. I heard that she died a few years later, and the younger children were looked after by Marks parents.

It was hard work running the farm, when your father went to fight in the war. Your mother and I did all we could to keep body and soul together for the family. Etienne was not well and was not able to do much to help, and as you know he passed away in 1947, three years after your own dear father.

When your parents got married, they took over the farm and we moved into Rose Cottage. Amongst the things we took with us from the farm, was the trunk I brought back from Russia when we left in 1919. It occurred to me that I had never sorted it out in all that time, after all it only had my uniforms in it and a few trinkets given to me by Madame. I thought it was time I checked the contents, partly to make sure there were no clothes moths coming into our new home. Etienne would not allow it in the house until I had checked, so it sat in the back garden for a couple of weeks. Thankfully it didn't rain and it didn't get damaged. When I opened up the trunk, it was like going back in time to another life. My uniforms and shoes still wrapped as I had left them, and two hats, which are sadly out of fashion now. At the bottom of the trunk I found a locked box. How it got there I had no idea, but it soon became apparent that Madame must have had it placed there before the trunk was shipped to my parents. Etienne removed the box from the trunk, it was quite heavy. There was a key in the lock which opened the door, where we found a note from Madame telling me that the key would only work on the inside locks if I pressed firmly on each lock as the key turned. I opened the main

122

section and I found a number of items all wrapped in newspaper, not the tissue paper that I would have used. The first item I unwrapped was a pearl and sapphire necklace, the next item an egg cup, I continued unwrapping and uncovered five more egg cups, a cruet set, a collection of enamelled coffee spoons, a tiara, earrings, a gold plate and, the pièce de résistance was one of Madame's treasured eggs. It is the one called The Hen in the Basket. I could not believe what I was seeing, all these treasures in my trunk, and I hadn't known they were there. The next thought I had was, what if people thought I had stolen them! But I should not have worried, as Madame in her wisdom had written me a letter to say she could not take everything with her, but she was not going to leave her precious items to the Bolsheviks who would not know their worth or the love poured into them from her beloved Alexander.

As you can imagine, these items were too fine for a common farmer and his wife to have, we could not use them, but neither did we want to sell them. Your grandfather and I decided that we would put the items in a safe and secure place and would leave them to you. I did keep some of the earrings to wear, but everything else is hidden away. I will leave you further instructions as to where.

The wren salts, as you know are passed down from first born to the next first born in each generation as a baptism gift. These were another of Madame's gifts. The rest of my story, you know.

May God truly bless you Albert,

Your loving Grand-mère x x x

Jenny sat amazed at the letter and wondered what had happened to the treasures from the box. She had never seen anything remotely resembling the list of items. She searched through all the other papers, reading each one. There was a copy of the deeds poll under Royal Licence which allowed the family surname to be changed from Oiseau to Bird, organised by the Dowager Empress as a final gift to Genevieve and Etienne enabling them to live in the country of their choosing without problems over a strange surname. Of the other papers, two were travel papers for Genevieve and Etienne, and the others were birth and marriage certificates. There was no further instruction from Genevieve to Albert giving the location of the bounty.

Jenny opened one of the drawers where she found an envelope with her name on it and the date of her twenty-first birthday. Opening the envelope, she found a letter from her grandparents. A tear leaked from her eye, as she recalled that her grandparents had died in a car accident six months before her twenty-first birthday.

To the most beautiful grand-daughter in the world.

Darling Jennifer, by now you will have read the letter that your great, great, grandmother, Genevieve wrote to grandad Albert telling him all about her life in Russia and the amazing things she was given by the Dowager Empress. As our only grand-child, we want to give you these items as an expression of our love for you. Perhaps, you will have more of an idea of what to do with them. We are in awe of the esteem that Genevieve was held in by the Dowager, and amazed at the generosity shown to her. We know how much you like puzzles and adventure, so have left you some clues as to the whereabouts of the items, have fun.

We wish you the most wonderful 21st birthday and hope that your life will be blessed with great riches.

Lots of love

Grandma and Grandad x

Jenny found it hard to take in that the Russian treasures from her great, great, grandmother, were now hers. This was truly mind-boggling. She tried to picture herself wearing a tiara and the pearl and sapphire necklace, but try as she might, she could only envisage it with jeans and a t-shirt – not very becoming. She looked through all the papers to see if she could see another envelope with her name on it, or something that might look like clues to the whereabouts of the hidden treasure, but could see nothing.

She tidied up the papers and put them back in the main section of the crimson box and told herself that she couldn't miss what she didn't know she had in the first place, but felt disappointed that she wouldn't be able to find the hidden items. Jenny got up and went to the kitchen to make another coffee and wondered what the egg looked like that the Dowager Empress had given to Genevieve. What she did know, was that it had contained a hen of some sort. Jenn knew, from the newspaper article she'd found under the fridge, that there were some eggs missing from the collection, so could only presume it was one of those. She knew there were some missing from the collection, so could only presume it was one of those.

She wandered back to the living room and as she sat down, noticed a small white card wedged between the side of the chair and the cushion. Retrieving it, she saw it was the same handwriting as that in the letter from her grandparents. It read

In the lining of my dome, in the bottom of my home.

Jenny found a notepad and pen from her parent's desk, and wrote the words down in bold at the top of the page underlining the words lining, dome, bottom and home. She tried to think of something with a dome that would have a lining but could only think of an igloo, which was unlikely to have a lining in the first place. 'What a ridiculous idea' Jenny told herself. She wondered if there had been anything in the attic that had a dome. She turned her thoughts to *bottom of my home*, 'well that would be the cellar', she said to herself and ran downstairs. There in front of her was the trunk with its domed lid. Of course, that was it.

She lifted the lid of the trunk and saw that it was lined with beautifully printed paper, cream with little pink rosebuds on it. The light wasn't bright enough to examine the lid properly, so she fished her mobile out of her pocked and switched on the torch app. The light swam over the lining of the lid, but Jenny could not see any rips or tears or anything to suggest that the lining had come away at any point. The torch light shone down the edges of the lid interior, still nothing. There was a central spine, which, when Jenny ran her hand over it, she could feel that it wasn't smooth. She examined the area more closely and could just see a very feint line where the paper had been cut and repasted. Jenny remembered seeing a sharp knife on the bar and fetched it. She managed to cut the paper, just inside the original cut mark, cutting round two sides only, to limit the damage to the lid. She pulled out a folded piece of paper, opened it up and read:

*Well done, that was an easy one, the clues will get harder, after all,
this is a treasure hunt!* Xx

Jenny read on to the next clue.

I used to be mined, where it can be quite wet,

but you'll find I'm a dry one, old, yes you bet.

If you're in the cellar, I'm really quite near.

It may be dark, but there's nothing to fear.

This was getting intriguing. Jenny went back upstairs with
the paper to sit in comfort in front of the fire. It was now
early evening and Jenny wondered if Michael would be back
soon.

She checked the answer machine for any messages, but
there were none. Dialling 1471 showed that no-one had
called. She wandered into the kitchen and made herself a
sandwich, and poured herself a glass of chardonnay, though
with all the excitement of what she'd found in the box, she
wasn't really very hungry. Her mind wandered back over
the events of the last twenty-four hours. Had Michael really

come back? Anger started to swell up inside her as she recalled the act of Michael boldly walking out for a short while. How dare he. Where was the man she'd fallen in love with? The man who was so thoughtful and considerate. She thought back to their last holiday in November 2014.

CHAPTER TWELVE

Jenny lay on her stomach leaning on her elbows as Michael gently rubbed sun protection cream onto her skin. He started at her feet and worked his way up her legs, ensuring that the lotion was absorbed by her skin just under her bikini.

'Umm, that feels so good. You should get a job as a masseuse' Jenny laughed.

'Not sure you'd like this service extended to others though would you?' Michael replied laughing, as his hands disappeared to ensure that the sides of Jenny's breasts were protected. 'I mean this is a pretty personal service I'm performing right now.'

Jenny was enjoying the impromptu massage and relishing the fact that Michael thought to extend the lotion under her clothing so that should she move or readjust her swimwear, she would not burn as she had on previous holidays. He was so thoughtful unlike previous boyfriends who would just dollop the lotion on and half-heartedly rubbed it over her skin.

'Now that I've finished, I hope Madame doesn't mind if I

go for a swim?'

'No you carry on Jeeves, I'm quite happy here with my puzzle book.' She waited for the gentle pat on her backside as Michael laughed and wasn't disappointed.

Michael had suggested the break having seen it advertised in the travel agent's window on his way home one evening.

'Can we afford it?

'It is in the winter sale, and we didn't exactly have good weather in the summer, did we?'

They had gone on a walking holiday in Northumbria and unsurprisingly, it had rained every day.

'I know you were disappointed in the summer and I just thought you'd enjoy it. You deserve it.'

Michael always knew the right things to say. He made her feel special and loved. He never stopped surprising her. There weren't many weeks that went by when he didn't buy her flowers or take out for dinner. It was his thoughtfulness, care and consideration that Jenny loved. She was at the forefront of all his decisions. If she'd had a demanding day at work, he would run a bath for her with lit candles around the edges and a glass of wine would appear as she sat luxuriating in the thick layer of bubbles. Jenny's welfare was at the base of everything. Many of her friends were amazed that the so-called honeymoon period hadn't fizzled out. They had warned her that after a few months, the arguments would start and excuses would start as to why he was late home or going out without her, but none of this had happened. Michael and Jenny understood each other, treated each other as equals and although they would have serious debates on issues, they never argued. Jenny had followed her parents example of married life, which was to always talk it out, not let it fester.

She recalled the same friends who, when Michael left, gave her the 'told you so' conversations. She tried to push these memories away as she remembered that her father was a member of the local history group that covered Wartlington and three of the surrounding villages and wondered if there were any books on the shelf about the village. She found a locally produced booklet which gave very scant information and told her nothing she didn't already know about the village. As she returned the booklet to its place on the shelf, the phone rang.

'Hi Jen, it's Michael.'

'Hi, is everything ok?' Jenny asked relieved to hear his voice.

'Yes, as far as I can see, the house doesn't look like it's been broken into, however, the bug I left in the phone has been removed and stamped on. I found it in the kitchen bin. I've replaced the bug, and I've left the broken one in the bin. Whoever got in, was very clever. I'm going to stay here tonight and tomorrow, I'll put in some security cameras and an alarm, so I may not be back until the day after. Will you be ok?'

Jenny's heart sank as he heard him say he wouldn't be back that evening.

'Oh my… you mean someone did break in? How?' Jenny felt panicked. She just knew someone had been in the house previously, now Michael had confirmed it.

'Err yes. They must have a duplicate key or be a confident lock picker.'

'Is the place in a mess?'

'No, which is why I didn't think at first, that anyone had been in the house. It was only when I went to put a piece of kitchen roll in the bin, that I found the broken bug, then I checked the phone. By the way, that was a very clever thing you did, putting a piece of paper in the door frame. I've checked all the rooms, and it was only the kitchen that seems to have been entered. Did you find anything interesting in the box?'

'Yes, I did, but I'll tell you all about it when you get back. If you're putting security cameras in, I guess you can remove my bits of paper.' She wasn't sure that she wanted to divulge everything to him.

Michael laughed 'already done. I'll hide cameras in all the rooms and connect them to my laptop, then if anyone does make a return visit, we'll be able to see who it is. Now remember, don't go out and don't answer the door. I'll ring you again tomorrow and let you know how I'm getting on. Love you.'

'I love you too, stay safe.' The phone clicked off, the call finished. Tears sprang to Jenny's eyes as she replayed in her mind Michael disappearing, coming back and leaving again. This just wasn't right.

With the prospect of an evening on her own Jenny turned on the television. There was nothing on but repeats. She left the set on, turned down the sound and picked up the notepad and the paper she had found in the trunk. There was another line she'd missed reading

If you're having trouble, I'll give you a clue

I lie twixt the church, the pub and the people.

That really didn't help at all. There was only a road between the pub and the church and if people was the cottages, well, still a road.

Jenny made a list of things that could be mined, especially in the UK. Coal, tin, oil, slate, limestone, gold, rock salt, probably a whole host of other things. Surely the only thing that might be wet from the list would be gold. She wondered what the geology was in the area, and searched on the internet. She found that limestone had been quarried extensively in the area for a couple of centuries. There were lime kilns all around the area, that had to be the answer.

Jenny surmised that lying between the church and the pub, must be a tunnel, not the road, either natural or man-made. If it was a tunnel, then there must have been an entrance in the cellar, but now that her father had renovated it, finding the entrance would be difficult without ruining all his handiwork. Presumably he'd never found an entrance, as he'd never mentioned it. Jenny went downstairs and looked around her father's bolt-hole. She walked about the floor, stamping her foot every now and then to see if there were any discernible changes in sound.

Thud, thud, thud.

The sound didn't change at all, even having moved the chairs about and stamping behind the bar, it was the same solid thud. Jenny opened the fridge and removed a tin of lemonade. Looking around her, the walls were all clad in tongue and groove wood panelling.

'Well I've stomped all over the floor' she said to herself 'I guess I can't lose anything by banging the walls.'

She started in the corner by the trunk, banging the wall in what she hoped was the same line around the room. By the time she was round the fourth side, her hand, understandably, was getting a little sore. Almost in the corner back by the trunk, there was a distinct change in the sound. Checking it wasn't just a sore hand and that she hadn't hit the spot with the same intensity, she used her other hand. There was a perceptible difference.

'Humph,' she exclaimed 'why didn't I go round the room the other way, it would have saved a lot of time.'

She examined the cladding and prodded each length of wood to see if there was a spring-actioned door. A sudden draft of cool air, told her she was right, as the door opened enough for her to get her hand behind it. She was greeted with the view of another door, with what she remembered were called barn latch handles, the same latches that were on all of the internal doors in the cottage. Jenny opened the door tentatively. It was very thick and heavy, and stopped most of the cool air seeping through. She peered into the darkness, but could not see a thing, though it did smell of damp. The air was cool, but not cold. Jenny pushed the door shut and took note of where the hidden door was in the cellar. She counted the strips of tongue and groove, the sixth one in from the corner.

CHAPTER THIRTEEN

Jenny filled a small bottle with water, before fetching her walking boots, jacket and a torch. In a desk drawer in the living room, Jenny remembered seeing a stick of chalk, which she fetched and wrapped in a sheet of kitchen paper and put in her jacket pocket along with a small notepad and pen. Happy she had everything she needed, including her mobile phone, which although she knew would not work underground, she took anyway and made her way down to the cellar. She counted the wooden strips and found the release point on the door. She propped it open with the fire extinguisher that was stored in the corner, just in case it shut and she couldn't get back in. With a sharp intake of breath, she opened the second door and checked it had a latch on the other side. Switching on the torch, she shone it over the back side of the door, then round the top of the steps.

She carefully navigated the steps, eight of them. Shining the torch off the walls, Jenny could see that it was naturally made. The roof of the tunnel wasn't high up, but gave enough room for people to walk around comfortably without banging their heads. The surface of the walls was smooth, probably from having water running over them.

Trickling down the centre of the floor was a thin stream of water. She tried to work out how deep the water must have been in the tunnel to allow access to the wells but not leak into the cellar.

There was the option of walking right or left. She turned right, marking an upwards arrow on the wall of the steps with the chalk. A small glimmer of light was shining down from up above which Jenny took to be light shining down from a disused well, probably the one in the garden. The tunnel floor gently sloped downwards in line with the hill, getting narrower the further she went. Jenny took the decision to turn around and walked past the steps of Rose Cottage.

Before long, the path had risen slowly before levelling out. After a few yards, there was a fork in the tunnel. Jenny placed an arrow facing the way she'd come with a 'H' underneath it. She turned to the left fork. It was a little uneasy underfoot in places, slippery more than anything, well worn. Not far along the passage were steps and the end of the tunnel. Jenny went up the steps carefully and quietly. Shining the torch at the roof, she saw a trap door, and could hear sounds above. She recognised the voice of Jim, the Landlord of the pub, and turned back down the steps and back to the fork.

Jenny carried on walking a further hundred yards before another set of stairs presented themselves. She didn't need to go up them as a cross on the wall indicated that it would be the church. Another hundred yards made another fork visible. Jenny marked the wall with an arrow and H and took the right fork. The ground gently rose upwards and another shaft of light shone down onto the ground. Another well-shaft, this one brought with it the unmistakable aroma of the slurry pit which meant she was heading for the farm house. Continuing up the passage, it came to an abrupt end with three steps up to a wooden door. Jenny knew the farmhouse well but could not fathom out where in the house the door would be. A question to ask her parents. As she shone her torch around the door frame, she noticed a rolled-up piece of paper in the door frame. She plucked it out and saw it had her name written on it. She put it in her pocket to look at back at the cottage.

She returned back to the fork and took the tunnel as yet unexplored. It went on for several hundred yards without any break in the roof for a well-shaft. The torch light picked out niches in the wall where perhaps items had been stored or people could hide unseen. 'Interesting' Jenny whispered. She wondered what the tunnels would have been used for. They must have held water at some point in the not too distant past for the wells to draw water from.

In the distance, Jenny heard two male voices having a heated discussion. Horror and panic filled her whole body. There were other people down here. What an idiot she was to think nobody else would use the tunnels. She turned back and walked as quickly and quietly as she could, hoping that the sound of her boots didn't echo. The voices appeared to be following and she heard a few words.

'We'll meet here again tomorrow at 10am. Don't be late.'

The voice was vaguely familiar, but it could be anybody she knew in the village. She picked up her pace trying to make it back to the steps of Rose Cottage but the footsteps were getting closer and she could see a torch light bouncing off the walls. Noticing one of the niche's in the wall, she darted into one of them and crouched down as low as she could at the back of it. One person walked past where she was hidden, the other person must have gone back. Jenny waited for a few minutes, listening. The footsteps were receding until finally she could hear nothing. She waited another couple of minutes to make sure it was safe to come out of hiding.

Reaching the top of the steps of the cellar for Rose Cottage, she stepped through the doorway and shut the door firmly and quietly as the motion sensor lights flicked into life. Jenny noticed the knife in the trunk that she had used to split the lining paper the day before. She picked it up and jammed it into the latch system which hopefully would stop anyone opening it and then firmly shut the inner door, but not before listening for the voices and footsteps. All was quiet, apart from Jenny's heart which was pounding so hard, she felt sure she could hear it. She walked over to the bar and poured herself a glass of water. She sat down in one of the chairs till her breathing and heartbeat settled back to somewhere near normal. The tunnels were in use by someone today. When she felt more relaxed, Jenny went upstairs to the living room where she fired up her laptop.

In the search engine, she entered *village tunnels*. There was an amazing list of villages which had tunnels underneath them, some were villages under villages. Several pages on, Jenny found Wartlington.

Legend has it that goods were brought to the pub in coaches and wagons from Shardlow on the River Trent. The tunnels were used to distribute these goods around the village. This was a precarious disposition as the tunnels often flooded with rainwater which supplied the wells and pumps in the village with their water. Legend also stated that the tunnels were used at the time of the Reformation to hide priests.

This Jenny could believe as there was a Priest Hole in one room at the farmhouse. There was an added note about the wells.

The spring that feeds the wells in the village is below floor of the tunnel. All wells have now been capped off after a health and safety report found traces of E.Coli, Salmonella and other Microsporidia were found in the water.

'Well, that's answered that query.' She said to herself and remembered the rolled-up piece of paper she had taken from the door frame. It was spotted with mildew and felt damp to the touch. She unrolled it gently and read the words it contained.

Right, centre, kneel down and pray.

Right must refer to the tunnel she'd taken at the fork from the farmhouse that she had followed before she'd first heard the voices. She resolved to go back down to the tunnel in an hours' time, when hopefully it would be free of other people, even though the thought of it filled her with dread. She checked the answer machine and noticed there was a message which when she played it was from Michael.

'Hi Jen, I presume you're in the shower or looking at items in the trunk. I'll be back tomorrow. The work is going well at the house. Lots of love, bye'.

Ashamedly, Jenny felt quite relieved that he wasn't coming home till the next day, it meant that she could go exploring in the tunnel without wondering if Michael would arrive home and find her missing. Remembering the work he said he'd been doing, she wasn't sure whether to tell him about the Russian treasures she had apparently inherited. Her wedding vows came to mind, how she'd promised to share everything she had with Michael but given his revelation that he hadn't been truthful about his working life seemed to put a different perspective on things.

Having made up her mind to go back down into the tunnel, Jenny decided that she should make sure her clothing was black or at least dark, so that if need be, she could blend into the shadows of the recesses more easily. She didn't own a dark jacket, so wandered into her parent's room to see if one of them had a jacket she could borrow. While looking in the wardrobe, she noticed what looked like a pair of swimming goggles, but when she picked them up, the lenses were strange. Putting them on, Jenny realised that they were night vision goggles and remembered her father's new hobby of watching bats. She decided to borrow them, so that she wouldn't need to use the torch so much.

Jenny's mother had a dark grey jacket, which would be just the job. Checking she had everything she needed, Jenny opened the inner door in the cellar, and as quietly as she could, removed the knife from the latch of the outer door. She had to wiggle it a bit, as she'd jammed it in the space quite hard. She listened carefully for any sounds on the other side then lifted the latch and pulled the heavy door open slowly, still listening for any movement. She put on the night vision goggles. The view in the tunnel was certainly different to that with a torch, and she waited a couple of minutes at the top of the steps, letting her eyes adjust to the view through the goggles. Jenny found her way down the steps, and headed left, then right, then left again. At the next fork, she took the turning as instructed and came to an abrupt end by some steps. This was also the point at which the trickle of water entered the tunnels.

'Could this be right' she thought to herself.

She stretched out her hand and worked her way across the wall, suddenly her hand was in fresh air and the tunnel diverted around a wall that was jutting out.

'Wow, nobody can see me now, unless they know about this part of the tunnel and come down it.' She whispered.

She carried on along the tunnel for about a hundred yards, before it came to a definite dead end. Centring herself in the middle of the floor, she knelt down, not sure what to do next. Jenny decided to lift the goggles up onto her forehead and dug the torch out of her pocket. She shone it along the wall and felt along it with her spare hand. She tried to remember the height of her grandfather, and reckoned he must have been a bit taller than herself, so raised the height of her search by a few inches. She almost immediately found a hole in the rock which looked like it had been home to some spiders. Thankful she was wearing gloves, she put her hand in the space and felt around. 'Hooray' she whispered and pulled out an envelope. She put her hand back in the crevice to make sure she hadn't missed anything, then did her best to rearrange some of the cobwebs over the entrance to the hole, just in case anyone did come down this way, and put the envelope and torch in her pocket, and pulled the goggles back down over her eyes.

Jenny was almost back to the split wall when she heard footsteps. Panicked, she tucked herself into the corner at the bottom of the outcropped wall, making herself fit into the space as best she could, and pulled the collar up on the jacket, over her head. The footsteps were coming towards her from the main tunnel, then stopped. A door opened, somewhere above her and a voice called down.

'Ollie, you need to come up, we said we'd meet tomorrow morning at ten.'

Jenny's heart felt like it stopped still. The voice belonged to Michael, she was willing to lay bets on it. Her heart suddenly pounded away in her chest, and she felt sure it must be loud enough to echo around the tunnel walls.

'OK M-M-Mark, I just thought I'd take a look around, this is the reason I want to b-b-buy the p-p-property.'

Jenny's mind raced. It couldn't be Michael, he was back at the home they had shared together, he'd not long left a phone message, so how could he be here in Wartlington and who was Ollie? More than that, if it was Michael, why was he being called Mark.

Whoever Ollie was, he went up the steps and Jenny heard the door shut with a loud thud and a grating noise that was possibly a bolt. She picked herself up off the floor and brushed the dust off her clothing. She had to get out of here in case they decided to come back. As she walked along the tunnel, she tried to work out how this Ollie thought he could buy the old priory, when her father resolutely refused to sell it.

Returning to the cellar, she stopped at each fork and rubbed the chalk mark off the walls. She didn't want anyone knowing that someone else had been down in these tunnels. Jenny shut the outer door firmly, ensuring the latch was caught in place, then shut the inner door and pushed one of the heavy chairs against it. She took off the night vision goggles and jacket and went upstairs to the kitchen where she emptied the pockets, made sure the jacket was dust free and took it upstairs to put away, with the goggles.

Once back downstairs, Jenny lit the fire, then made herself a coffee. She felt shook up and unnerved, shocked and exhilarated all at the same time.

'Is this what Michael feels like when he's working, chasing villains around Europe' she mused.

She decided to hide all the papers that made reference to her being given the treasures from her great, great, grandmother. At this point in time, she wasn't sure if telling Michael all about them, would be the best idea, especially if he was actually in Wartlington and not at home like he said he would be. She wondered where to put the papers and remembered that one of the rafters in her bedroom had a hidey hole in it, one that she had told nobody about, so they should be safe there. Before taking the papers upstairs, she opened the newly retrieved envelope. It was covered in cobwebs and had a bit of mildew on it, but there was her name on the front of it. There was a folded paper inside which she took out and found another folded paper inside it.

Dear Jenny, if you are reading this, then well done. We hope you enjoyed your treasure hunt. You may have gathered that the 'treasure' is not actually in the tunnels though they are a means to getting to it. We split the items up into three lots, so that, should anybody come across it before you, you wouldn't lose the lot, although with the letters and everything else, you have proof that the goods belong to you. So here are the three final clues for you. Lots of love Grand ma and

Grandad xx

Jenny wasn't sure if she could take any more of this so-called excitement, but unfolded the other paper from the envelope anyway and read the clues.

You'll find me in water, its source has run dry.

You'll need to go down then up to the sky.

Count twenty and two and one more for good luck,

then look all about you for the pigs that can fly.

You'll find me in a guarded place,

among the sticks and stones.

A place where birds find their rest.

The wren it is the best.

You'll find me in a little place of sanctuary,

in the place that is waiting for someone to play.

Hidden away from all those that seek,

in a hole that isn't a hole. (We couldn't get it to rhyme).

Jenny didn't like the sound of the first clue, it sounded like she'd have to go back down in the tunnels, and with other people roaming about down there, she wasn't sure it was a good thing. She did, however, have until 10am the next morning to go back down, hopefully without being seen or found.

'Why isn't life simple' she said out loud. 'OK boots, where are you, we're going back down, though I guess I ought to make sure I know where I'm going.'

Jenny read over the clue again, down then up in a dry water source. It could only be one place, the well in the garden. She knew she couldn't go down the well, as her father had cemented a grill in place to stop anyone accidentally falling down it.

'Right Jen, fetch your torch and your waterproof, because no matter how dry the bottom is, all that snow on top has had to go somewhere and the walls will be wet.'

Jenny removed the chair from against the door, and opened both the inner and outer doors, listening out for anyone who may be in the tunnel. All was quiet. She went down the steps and turned right. If she was correct, the first shaft of light should be the well in the garden. She hadn't given thought as to how she was going to climb up the well sides, but she shouldn't have worried as there was a metal ladder inches away from the shaft walls. She gingerly stepped into the space of the well shaft, hoping that it had been capped off with something that wouldn't rot or give way. She counted each rung as she went up.

'one, two, three… twenty-one, twenty-two and one for good luck.'

The ladder was in good condition, although a little slippery in places where moss had settled and snow had dripped. It was also very cold, and she wished she'd remembered to put on her gloves. Hanging on with one hand, she took the torch back out of her pocket, wishing she had one of those head torches she'd seen advertised in magazines, or even worn her father's night vision goggles. She looked up, no flying pigs overhead. Next, she scraped the sides of the walls with the edge of the torch to get rid of some of the moss and algae which fell to the ground beneath her, still nothing. Jenny went over the clue in her head.

'Blast, it's the wrong well.'

Her parents had been living at the farm and her grandparents had lived in Rose Cottage. She climbed back down the ladder kicked the debris she'd scraped off the walls to the side of the tunnel and nervously found her way through the passages to the farm's well shaft. She went through the motions of scraping the walls when suddenly beaming back at her was a flying pig carved into one of the bricks.

'Ok Mr pig, what are you hiding?'

Jenny stuck the torch between her teeth to free up her hand to feel round the brick, whilst hanging onto the ladder with her other hand. Scraping away a layer of mud from the grouting, the brick moved easily.

'Oh heck, what am I supposed to do with you now, I haven't got enough hands.'

Jenny remembered that she had a carrier bag in her pocket, she always carried one in her waterproofs in case she came across fruit and such like on her walks. She managed to manoeuvre the brick into the bag and slipped her arm through the handles. There was a hole behind the brick which she bravely stuck her hand into and felt about.

'Eeek'

There was something slimy in there. The thought of slimy creatures mixed with the smell from the slurry pit was making her feel nauseous. She gritted her teeth and reached in again. The something slimy had substance and was, she was relieved to find, a box covered in very thick polythene. She managed to get the object out of the hole, place it in the bag and put the brick back into place, muttering as she did so.

'As much as I like puzzles, dear grandparents, why didn't you just put the lot in a safety deposit box at the bank?'

Looking up at the sky, dark clouds were passing overhead, and the odd spot of water was landing on her head. Jenny switched off the torch and stuffed it back in her pocket and gingerly made her way down the ladder. As she approached the bottom of the shaft, she stopped and listened out for any voices or footsteps. Nothing being heard, she continued down. There were bits of moss and mud on the ground which Jenny kicked into the trickle of water running down the centre of the tunnel and returned to the safety of the cellar.

Her boots and coat were filthy. There was no way she could march across the carpet and up to the kitchen without leaving dirty marks everywhere. Standing still, she took off her coat and folded it inside out, placed it on the floor to the right of the door, then stood on it, closed both doors and took her boots off. Standing on the carpet, she picked her coat and boots up, scooped up the carrier bag and went upstairs. In the kitchen, she sponged down her coat, then cleaned her boots under the tap.

'That's far too much excitement for one day, time to stoke the fire, make tea and have a drink.' Jenny said to the polythene encased box. 'You can wait until after I've eaten. After all, you've waited all this time to be discovered, so another hour or two won't hurt you.'

The phone rang. Jenny checked her breathing as she answered it, she wanted to appear normal, whatever that meant, when she spoke to Michael.

CHAPTER FOURTEEN

'Hi Jen, have you had a good day?'

'Michael, so glad you called, I've been missing you. How's the work going?'

'Well I have the camera's in and the alarm fitter is calling in the morning, so hopefully I'll be home for tea. Is there anything you want me to bring with me, food or drink, milk?'

'A pint of milk would be good, the milk in the fridge is smelling a little dodgy, probably because we don't drink much of it. Oohhh and something yummy like a cream doughnut and a bar of my favourite chocolate.'

Michael laughed, 'you don't change do you? Would you like a bottle of fizz, save your dad's supply?'

'Mmmm, that would be nice, perhaps a couple of bottles?'

'I was right, you don't change at all. What's the weather like there?'

'If you are actually in the village' she thought to herself, 'you'd know.'

'It was raining earlier, I haven't looked outside for a while. What's it doing there?

'Just the same, though it is still raining. Just going down to the take-away for something to eat, so as long as everything goes well, I'll be home for tea tomorrow. Love you lots, bye'

'Love you too, bye.' She'd said the words, but wasn't sure how much she still believed in them.

Jenny put the receiver down, and drew all the curtains. After throwing a small log on the fire, she sat down with the package she had retrieved from the well shaft. She had cut the polythene packaging off in the kitchen which revealed a shoe box wrapped in twenty-first birthday paper, tied together with a silver ribbon. The box sat on the coffee table while Jenny pulled the ribbon open and lifted the lid. Everything in the box was individually wrapped in birthday paper. The first item she unwrapped was a cruet set for salt, pepper and mustard on a very ornate stand. The next item was two rings. One held a large sapphire surrounded with diamonds, the other was a large ruby, set with small rubies. The third package revealed the hair comb that Genevieve had described in one of her letters. It was exquisite, roses made up of yellow diamonds, emeralds and small garnets. The fourth and last item was a gold chain, not a single strand, but four in varying lengths.

Jenny sat back against the chair, looking at the items she had just unwrapped. Just one of these items would have been incredible on its own, but all of this, was amazing. She had no idea where to put them, to keep them safe. She decided that the best way to hide them, was out in the open as if they had always been there. She placed the cruet set in her mother's glass cabinet, it looked like it belonged. The rings and the gold necklace she took upstairs and placed in her jewellery box. The hair comb, she placed in the bottom drawer of the crimson leather box.

Jenny looked back at the other two clues. They weren't too hard to work out. The third clue she decided must be the priory which must contain a priest hole somewhere in the building. This was going to be the difficult one. There were over twenty-five rooms in the building on three floors, not including the attic.

The second clue sounded like sticks and stones may break my bones, which made her think of the family crypt across the road at the church and the words where birds find their rest, clinched it. This shouldn't be too hard. Jenny made the decision to visit it in the morning. She spent the rest of the evening watching a DVD with a glass of chardonnay for company.

When Jenny woke the next morning, it was dry, cold and breezy. She waited till 9am before ringing the vicarage.

'Hello Rector, Jenny Bird calling from across the road, how are you?

'Hello Jenny, I'm well, thank you for asking, and yourself?'

'Yes fine, just doing a bit of house-sitting for mum and dad while they gallivant around the Mediterranean for a few weeks. While I'm here I'm doing some research into the family history and wondered if you have a key to the family crypt?'

'Ahh, yes, I do have a key somewhere, but if I remember correctly, your father keeps his key on his garage key ring.'

Jenny looked up at the garage key hanging by the telephone and noticed a second key. 'Of course, I can see it now, sorry to have disturbed you Rector, thank you.'

'Don't worry Jenny, glad to help. Hope you find the

information you're after. Bye'

Next, Jenny texted her father.

Hi dad, hoping you're both having a great time. Rain here. Quick question, do you know if the priory has any priest's holes? Please txt back, don't ring. Love to you both, Jen xx

She didn't expect a quick response, but hoped it came before Michael got back.

Jenny waited until 10am, when she knew that the two men, Mark and Ollie, would be busy in the tunnels, doing whatever it was they were doing. As she opened the front door, she grabbed the garage key, checked for a third time that she had her mobile phone and picked up a large shopping bag in which she'd placed a pad of paper and a pen. She looked left and right to see if there was anybody about, then shut the door behind her.

Warily, she crossed the road to the church, checking around her as she went. She opened the gate, a lovely old lych-gate with a giant camellia tree, it was too big to be called a bush, growing next to it, covered in buds, waiting for the next few weeks to go by before the flowers opened. The gate gave a little creak as it both opened and closed. The path went up to the main door of the church and forked off round the back to the main churchyard. There were three or four family crypts here belonging to the long-standing families from the village. The crypt belonging to the Bird family was one of the two larger ones. The crypt was flanked on each side of by angels blowing trumpets guarding two wrought iron gates. Leaves had blown up against the bottom of the gates like a draught curtain protecting the inhabitants inside. The key was already in Jenny's hand ready to insert into the lock. It turned easily and Jenny pulled the gate open, stepped inside and pulled the gate behind her.

She looked about her and counted eleven caskets. Eight adults which Jenny could identify and three very small ones, the dates on two of them could be linked to her grandparents and her great grandparents, babies who had died in infancy. The third had no name, or date, but what it did have was a wren sitting on a branch carved into the stonework. Jenny was taken aback, did her grandparents intend for her to open a casket? She checked the other ledges. There was nothing else that she could see with a wren on, besides this small casket. Her grandparents remains were in the crypt and she spoke to them, as if they could hear.

'Well granny and gramps, I hope you're having a good laugh, wherever you are. You obviously had great fun putting this whole thing together, and I do wish you were here to see me sorting this out. But are you serious about me opening up this casket?' No reply, not unexpected. 'Ok, on your head be it.'

Jenny was surprised that nobody had questioned the appearance of the casket when her grandparents were laid to rest. She examined the lid and gently pushed it to see how easy it might be to move it. She could feel it give, but it didn't move much. Jenny put the bag she was carrying down on the ground, and placed the key in her pocket. She placed a hand at either end of the lid and lifted it. It was very heavy and didn't stay in the air long, landing with a bang.

'Sorry everyone' Jenny said out loud 'I'll try to be quieter. Perhaps if I push the lid... Yay, that worked.'

Jenny tentatively peered into the space below. The only thing she saw, with relief, was a large polythene covered box, slightly bigger than the one she had found in the well. She managed to move it out of the casket without the lid moving any further. Having placed the package in her shopping bag, Jenny pulled the lid back into place and pushed the casket as far back on the ledge as she could. A noise behind her made her jump. She looked up. The gate had closed and self-locked. Just as well she had the key in her pocket. She made a note of the details from the two small caskets. There was the sound of someone walking along the path from the front of the path.

'Hello Jenny' a voice called out.

'Hi Rector, I don't suppose you could unlock the gate for me, if I pass you the key, it shut behind me.'

'Yes, of course, not a problem. Did you find all the information you wanted?'

'Yes, yes I did thank you. Going back home now to put the info in my record sheet.'

'Good, good, keep up the good work. Here's your key.'

The Rector carried on walking along the path while Jenny returned home with a heavy shopping bag.

She was beginning to feel like a renegade, creeping about the village recovering items from various places. She opened the front door checking there was nobody about watching her. With the door firmly closed, the garage key was hung back in its rightful place. Jenny took the shopping bag through to the kitchen and placed the package onto the kitchen table. She cut away the outside packaging and found a shoe box covered in the same twenty-first birthday paper.

There were six individual packages, which when Jenny opened them, contained six gold or silver egg cups, perhaps silver with gold linings; a pearl and sapphire necklace; a set of enamelled coffee spoons; a selection of earrings, with diamonds, rubies, garnets, emeralds and sapphires; a string of pearls and the most beautiful tiara, decorated with diamonds and emeralds. She sat looking at them with incredulity. If this was the result of the second package, what was the third going to hold? The egg cups were put in the glass cabinet on the bottom shelf along with the coffee spoons. The jewellery was far too elaborate to put in her jewellery box. Jenny looked to see if there was room in the hidey hole in the rafter in her bedroom. It all fitted in except for the tiara.

'Oh pants, where can I put you, that won't draw attention?'

She went down to the cellar, opened the trunk, lifted the hat box out and pulled the cloche hat out from the safety of the broad brimmed hat. Placing the tiara on top of the cloche, she returned it to its resting place and put the hats back in the box. Having put the lid down, she walked over to the door opened it and listened for any sounds through the outer door. In the distance, she could hear muffled voices and feet moving along the tunnel. Jenny shut the door and for extra safety, pulled another chair over to the door in the hope that two chairs would prevent anyone entering the cellar. She returned to the living room and tried to make it look like she had spent the last two days lounging in there doing nothing in particular. It wasn't too hard, she had the cryptic crossword book, television, DVDs and a book she was reading.

Jenny emptied the ash pan from beneath the grate before lighting a new fire. She opened the back door of the cottage and found the ash bucket her father filled before using its contents around the garden. Making sure she had locked the back door, Jenny lit the fire and noticed that there weren't many logs left. There was nothing for it, she would have to venture down the garden to the wood store. As a precaution, she locked the kitchen door behind her and took the panier down to the end of the garden. Over the hedge, in the car park, she could hear a conversation going on.

'Why have you been trampling down the tunnel at the far end?'

The voice sounded like Michael.

'I haven't.'

This voice belonged to the mysterious Ollie.

'Well someone's been down there. There's a chalk mark on the side of the wall with an arrow'

'Well, it w-w-wasn't m-m-me.'

Jenny stopped in her tracks. She'd missed one of the chalk marks. What an idiot. She stood still until she heard them get into a car and drive off. She quickly filled the pannier with logs and ran as best she could back to the kitchen with the awkward load. The door wouldn't open.

'Idiot, you locked it' she scolded herself and fumbled in her pocket for the key.

There were enough logs to last till Michael got back, though if he was in the pub carpark right now, he could be back at the cottage any time. She locked the door and went through to the living room with the panier. 'What's going on? What are we getting mixed up in? Michael, it's time you got back, I don't think I can cope.'

Jenny, who had been dozing on the settee, was woken up by her mobile phone buzzing, letting her know that she had a text message. It was from her father.

Hi Jen, we're having a wonderful time, wall to wall sunshine. Re your question about the Priory, there are possibly four priest's holes. One in the attic at the gable end facing the farm house. One on the 2ⁿᵈ floor, fourth room from the left at the back of the house. The third one is on the 1ˢᵗ floor, 5ᵗʰ room from the right at the front of the house and the fourth one, if I remember correctly, is in the ground floor near the entrance door. Hope that helps. Your mum sends her love, as do I xx

'Oh heck, four' exclaimed Jenny, 'the missing package could be in any of them.' She tried to think back to when she played in the building, and if there was any particular place she played in more than any of the others, but couldn't think of any. What she needed was a plan of action, an excuse for being in the building, not that she really needed an excuse, but she wanted to sound plausible should she bump into anyone. She stopped herself short.

'Why do I need an excuse? Dad owns it. The reason for anybody else being there needs to come from them.'

Jenny found her notebook and pen, and after putting on her jacket and boots, picked up the key and set off for the Priory. She walked confidently down the garden path and up to the lane, and along to the corner where the farm and priory kept an eye on each other. She opened the gate to the priory drive and walked down the path to the main door. Fetching the key out of her pocket Jenny was relieved to find that the door was locked. She pushed the door open and looked around. The first room on her right, was the old refectory and where the sun was shining through the window, she could see particles of dust, dancing in the air. The flagstone floor was damp, not surprising as nobody had lived here for goodness knows how long. The refectory table was still there, pushed up against the far wall. A couple of benches were stored underneath it, waiting for new inhabitants to come and make use of it.

Jenny returned to the hallway and entered the second door on the right. This was the back of the building and at one time, housed the kitchen. A huge chimney dominated the end wall, with an inglenook fireplace underneath it. Looking up into the chimney space, Jenny could see the old spit-roast arms that would hold meat, pots or kettles. Looking up into the dark void, she felt sure she could smell soot. To the side of the inglenook was a wooden door, which Jenny knew hid a stairway. The steps were made of stone and each one had a worn dip in the middle where countless feet had trodden over the centuries.

The first and second floors each had a corridor through the middle with six rooms each side of the corridor and each side of the central staircase, making 24 rooms in total. Each one just big enough for a bed or mattress and a prayer desk which were still evident in one or two of the rooms. The prayer desk was a very simple affair. It looked like a wooden step with an upright supporting another step. They didn't look very comfortable, but anything had to be better than kneeling directly on the wooden or stone slab floor.

Jenny counted the rooms, locating the fifth one from the right at the front of the house, and entered. She shut the door behind her and looked about the room. Directly opposite the door was a window. It had a deep ledge, as did all the windows in the building. If it hadn't been made of stone, it would have been an ideal hiding place. She walked around the small space, trying to detect any change in sound from her footsteps. As she approached the window, there was a discernible difference. She knelt down and inspected the floorboards. There was a knot in one of the boards that butted up to the wall. Jenny dug her fingernail into the edge of it, which dislodged the knot from its resting place revealing a finger sized hole, which when Jenny hooked her finger into it, she managed to lift floorboards in a space, not much bigger than a large shoebox. She shone her torch into the void. It went down into the space between the two floors and back towards the window. Lying down, Jenny pushed her arm back under the floor as far as it would go, but could not feel anything. She took her mobile out of pocket and switched on the camera, stuck her arm back into the space and took a couple of pictures, turning her hand round to hopefully capture different views. Pulling her arm back through, she inspected the photographs.

Wow, amazing, there's enough space for someone to sit crouched in there.'

It looked like the stone block had been hollowed out. 'How ingenious' she said to herself. It didn't look as if there was anything hidden in there. Jenny carefully replaced the floorboards and the knot and left the room.

Next Jenny turned to the central stairway and went to the second floor and opened the door of the room fourth from the left at the back of the house. The window in this room was high up, giving light, but not a view. Shutting the door behind her, she studied the floor and walls. There were no floorboards with knots in, and the back wall sounded solid. She tapped the walls, no change in sound.

'I wonder if Dad remembered the correct room' she mused.

She sat down on the dusty floor and tried to think out of the box. 'If I were putting in a hidey hole I didn't want discovered, where would I put it?'

Jenny decided it would be impossible to put anyone in a hole higher up, but what about at floor level? She crawled around the room on her hands and knees tapping the walls as she went. The wall between the third and fourth rooms did sound slightly different, but not much. The wall that the door was attached to, however, did make her heart leap. On reflection, the wall was slightly deeper than she was expecting, and she managed to prise the bottom of the wall away from its fixing to reveal a space long enough for someone to lie down with their legs pulled up. It couldn't have been very comfortable, and the person hiding would have to be very slim. She shone the torch into the space, which showed only cobwebs and mouse droppings. Having taken a photograph, she carefully replaced the section of wall, banging it back into place on the corner.

Jenny made her way to the attic and the gable end facing the farm. There wasn't a lot of light up there. Most of the windows were at the other end of the space. In the middle of the floor about three foot in from the gable end, Jenny could see that the floorboards had been cut indicating to anybody that there was a possible space underneath it. She managed to lift one of the boards and indeed there was space for two people to hide in relative comfort. But surely this was too obvious. It must have been a false hole, to show anyone hunting the priests, that they weren't aware that the priests holes should be more covertly hidden or that no-one was actually hidden there.

Jenny turned her attention back to the gable wall. The rafters that held the roof, were all thick wooden affairs that came down to ground level. With care, Jenny reasoned to herself, one could walk or straddle the rafter. She straddled the first rafter, and inched her way up it, holding on very carefully by hugging it. Half way up, there was a cavity. Jenny let go of the rafter with one hand and reached for her phone to take a photo. The flash was very bright and it dazzled her eyes. She blinked a few times to get rid of the flash. Managing to look at the photo she'd just taken, she could see that the cavity was long enough for a person to lie down and deep enough not to be seen. She couldn't see how anyone could logically hide in it though. Perhaps it had been used to hide things in, rather than people. There was nothing in this hole either. Putting her phone safely back in her pocket, Jenny inched her way back down to floor level.

There was just one place left to look and that was near the main door. Jenny brushed herself down and looked around the rest of the attic. At the far end, there must have been a hole in the roof as she could see that water had got in and the floor board underneath the gap was rotten. She made a note in her notebook, to remind her to tell her father. Jenny decided that perhaps she ought to check all the rooms in case there was other work that needed doing.

Back down on the second floor, third room from the right at the front, one of the windows was broken and the fifth room from the right at the back showed signs of the water permeating through the rotten floorboard above into the ceiling.

The first floor didn't show up any signs of work that needed doing. The ground floor also seemed in good condition, though the outside door in the back room on the left-hand side looked like it didn't shut properly.

'Perhaps the frame is warped' Jenny thought to herself. For such an old building, it was in very good repair.

It came to mind that Jenny hadn't seen anywhere on the ground floor that would lead to a cellar or the tunnel. She couldn't imagine that a flagstone would be lifted every time anybody wanted to access a cellar or tunnel. There must be an entrance somewhere. The only place she hadn't searched was the entrance hall. The central stairs were stone, but had been encased in dark square panelling at some point in more recent years, by which she meant the last hundred or so years.

Jenny examined both sides of the stairway, but could see nothing out of the ordinary. Recalling how the crimson leather box revealed its secrets by pushing the door, she began to push each panel to see if a door would spring open. She hadn't pressed many before the side of the stairway opened up. She stepped back in a panic and looked around her for a place to hide. What if she hadn't activated it, but someone coming up the steps from the tunnel? She ran through to the Kitchen and stood inside the fireplace where she couldn't be seen. There was silence, Jenny stepped out of her hiding place and returned to the stairway pulling the doorway open further to reveal a trap door. It was bolted shut, which told her that there was nobody down there at present. Before shutting the hidden door, she counted the panels to fix the location where she had pressed to open it in the first place. Third from the wall, third from the floor. 'Well that should be easy to remember' she thought. and wrote 3x3 in her notebook.

Jenny turned her attention to the main door in the hallway but before she could start examining the space, the door began to open. Jenny felt panicked, and quickly reminded herself that she had every right to be in the building and that whoever was trying to gain entry, was the interloper. She stood back and looked expectantly at the doorway as the door opened wide. The man who had opened it looked totally shocked to see her stood there.

'Hello, can I help you?' Jenny asked.

'Er, yes, er, no. W-w-what are you d-d-doing in here? This is m-m-my p-p-property' he replied

'Actually' Jenny countermanded, 'you will find this property belongs to my father and has been in our family for four generations. And what I am doing here is firstly none of

176

your business, and secondly, if you really want to know, I am carrying out an inspection of work that needs doing ready for the insurance.'

'Y-y-young lady, I b-b-bought this p-p-property two weeks ago from the f-f-farmer over there' he stuttered while pointing back towards the farm house.

'Wrong, the farmer over there is a tenant farmer and owns none of the buildings in this village. Perhaps you'd like to see the title deeds. If you have, as you insist, purchased this building from the farmer over there, can I suggest that you go and get your money back, because you have been conned.' Summoning up what confidence remained, she went on 'Now kindly give me the key, heaven only knows where you got it from, and get your ass off my property before I call the police.' As she pulled her mobile out of her pocket, the man dropped the key and ran.

Slamming the door behind him, Jenny sank to her knees with tears springing down her cheeks. She felt drained. It had taken all her nerves to hold her stand against him. Shaking, she stood up, opened the door and locked it behind her. All thoughts of looking for the fourth priests hole gone from her mind. She managed to get back home and shut herself in.

'This is torture' she decided 'what am I doing?'

Jenny was still shaking when she sat down at the kitchen table. Michael was due back within the next three hours, if he'd been away at all, that was, and not hidden himself away in the village. Jenny was not sure what to think. He'd been out of her life for just over a year without leaving any word and had walked back into it as if he'd been away for a couple of months. Where once she would have trusted him with her life, she now wondered if she knew anything about him after all.

The man purporting to be the owner of the priory sounded very much like the man called Ollie from the tunnel. He had looked vaguely familiar, but Jenny could not think where she may have seen him before. He wasn't a villager, of that she was sure. He was of average height and build, approximately 5' 9", with dark brown hair and green eyes. He was dressed in jeans, trainers and a navy fleece zipped up to the top. His hands were bare though she had noticed that his finger nails were bitten down almost to the quick, and she presumed he was of a nervous disposition which was likely why he'd stuttered when speaking to her. Then she remembered, he'd been in the library asking for books on villages in the middle of England. He'd certainly run off quickly when she'd produced her phone. Jenny remembered the key he'd dropped in his haste to get away and fetched it from her coat pocket. She laid it beside the key that belonged to her father. It was very similar, and gave the appearance of being well used.

Jenny's mobile buzzed, indicating an incoming text. Picking the phone up she swiped her finger over the scanner. As the phone opened up, she saw that she had inadvertently taken a picture of the interloper. As the flash must have gone off, there was a blurred image of his hand being raised to his face, but she could still see most of his features. The text was from her father.

Hi Jen, just remembered where the fourth p.hole is. There is a wooden cupboard built into the wall as you enter the hall, on the left. It is an old linen chest. The drawers don't open, they appear to be locked with the key missing. However, the base shelf of the cupboard lifts up providing a generous space for someone to hide. Love dad x

Jenny had forgotten all about the fourth hole, and now she knew where it was without having to search for it. She would have to bide her time until she could return to the priory to search the space. She remembered that the cupboard space above the drawers had been a favourite hiding place when she was younger, playing hide and seek with her friends.

Jenny had taken photographs of all the objects she had found on her treasure hunt, and decided to store them on a memory card. She had a cloud account, but couldn't be sure that Michael didn't have access to it. Having made sure everything she wanted to keep from her phone was transferred to the card, she removed it and taped it to the inside of the breadbin where it couldn't be seen. Next, she deleted all emails and text messages on the phone, clearing the recent history. She was taking no chances as to whether or not she could trust Michael. It wasn't long after sitting down, having made sure that everything she didn't want Michael to see was hidden away, that he arrived back. She heard a key in the front door then Michael called through.

'Hi Jen, I'm back'

Jenny didn't remember giving him a front door key, perhaps he'd picked a spare one up off the key rack by the telephone as he left.

'Oh good, I've missed you' she said as she got up off her

chair. 'I'm getting low on logs and as you told me not to go out…' she laughed.

'Is that all you've missed me for? Michael looked at her with a quizzical gaze, then grinned broadly. 'Ok, I'll get you some logs in before I take my coat off and refill the coal.'

'Did you have a good journey?' Jenny asked.

'Yes, wasn't bad, the toll road was closed due to an accident, and getting round Birmingham was a little busy, but other than that, fine. Here's your shopping, by the way.' He handed her a supermarket carrier bag.

'Ohhhhh lovely two cream doughnuts, I take it you'd like one of them?'

'Of course.'

'With a coffee?'

'Yes please, that would be lovely. I'll clean the ash pan out first.'

'No need, the ash bin is just outside the kitchen door, so I did do that' Jenny looked sheepishly at Michael. 'I know you said not to go out, but I didn't think that would count.'

She didn't tell him she'd been out a couple of other times, and that she had ventured into the tunnels.

Coffee made, shopping put away, logs and coal replenished, they were soon sat in front of a lit fire eating the doughnuts.

'So, what was in the box?'

'Oh, not a lot really. A couple of birth certificates, a deeds poll for the change of surname for my great, great grandparents, and the comb given to Genevieve.' Jenny hoped she sounded convincing. 'What about home? Is the alarm system in?'

'Yes, the chap was very prompt, here's the code' Michael fished into his jeans pocket and produced a business card with the four-figure code written on the back. 'It's very easy to use. When you leave the house, you punch in the number and press the button with the house symbol on it, and the same when you return.'

'What about the security cameras?

'They're ones I use in my job, all connected to my laptop. If anyone does go back, I'll be able to see everything that goes on. Though of course they now have to get past the alarm.'

It all sounded very matter of fact. Jenny noticed that Michael had changed his clothes, but none of it was from his wardrobe at home, which puzzled her. She hadn't been able to bring herself to clear his belongings out, mainly in the hope that one day he would come back. It wasn't as if he'd put on weight, or lost any, his clothes would fit him fine.

'I see you bought steaks' Jenny said. 'You cooking them?'

'Of course, thought you needed spoiling after a couple of days on your own again. Which is why I also bought the chocolate fondants for dessert.'

'What chocolate fondants? There weren't any in the bag.'

'Oh, they must have fallen out, I'll go and get them.'

Michael got up and went out of the front door. He returned ten minutes later with both the fondants and their wedding album.

'Just as well I'd forgotten them, I left the album in the boot as well. I thought you'd like to see it.'

Jenny took the album off him as he went to the kitchen to put the dessert in the fridge. So he had been home for some time at least. She was already leafing through the pages when Michael returned to sit down. There weren't many from the day itself, but Jenny's mother had organised a party a few weeks later, and brought in a photographer to record the event. As Jenny turned the next page, she was dismayed to see that a photograph had been ripped out. It was one of her and Michael signing the register, now it was missing.

'The photograph, it's missing.' She exclaimed, stating the obvious. She looked at Michael, with tears in her eyes. 'Did you do that?' she asked accusingly.

'No, no of course not' he sounded offended that she could think such a thing. 'Perhaps that's what our intruder came in for.' It sounded plausible, but why would anyone take a photograph of the pair of them? Michael was just as surprised as Jenny to see a picture missing.

When they went to bed that evening, Jenny feigned a headache, rebuffing all advances from Michael. She wasn't sure how she felt about him anymore and didn't feel willing to partake in any love-making. Jenny woke early the next morning, a little worried how Michael might have taken her refusal to his advances the night before. She needn't have worried, he was already up and dressed. Jenny showered and dressed, adding a fleece jumper to her layers, it seemed a little colder than it had been for a while. Reaching the kitchen, Michael was busy making breakfast and turned around to smile at her.

'Did you sleep well?

'Yes, much better knowing you were safely back'

'Look, you've been cooped up in the house for days, now I'm back, why don't you go for a walk and get some fresh air?

'That would be great. You coming too?

'No, as much as I would enjoy your company, I'll light a fire and get the house feeling a little warmer for when you get back.'

After breakfast, Jenny put on her walking boots, jacket and gloves, and ensuring she had some money in her pocket, set off on her walk. At the top of the hill, she turned left towards the shops and purchased a bar of chocolate and some new batteries for her torch. She didn't plan on walking far, just to the Rectory. Not wanting to be seen by

Michael, Jenny walked up the church path, round the back of the church, through the churchyard and past the crypts. The path carried on round to the back door of the vicarage. It was a favoured entrance by some of the locals who didn't want to be seen visiting the Rector. There was a door-bell which Jenny pressed. She was greeted by the Rector's wife.

'Hello Mrs Allen, sorry to bother you. Is the Rector in?'

'Hello Jenny, lovely to see you. Yes, Derek's in his study. Come in dear, are you keeping well? Are your parents enjoying their holiday? Would you like a cup of tea?'

'Er, yes, yes and yes please' Jenny replied in answer to the questions.

'Go on through to his study dear, I'll bring you a tea in a jiffy. DEREK,' Mrs Allen shouted, 'visitor for you.'

As Jenny approached the study door, the Rector opened it.

'Aahh Jenny, how lovely to see you again, do come in, take your coat off, have a seat. The study was small. Along one wall was a floor to ceiling bookcase, crammed with theological books and various versions of the Bible. A large desk overflowing with paperwork sat in the corner by the window. The only heating was a gas fire by the door. In the middle of the floor, taking up what space was left, was a coffee table and two kitchen style chairs. Now what can I do for you?'

'Well, this is going to sound strange, but, do you know if the vicarage or the church has any priests' holes or if there are any tunnels under the buildings? I read recently that Wartlington was used for smuggling or some such and that some of the buildings, especially the priory had priests' holes.'

'Goodness,' the Rector replied, 'well now let's see. I'm not aware of any priests' holes in either the Rectory or the Church, but, I do know about a tunnel. From what I recall being told when we first came here, there is a cross on the wall below the church, but, the access isn't from the church, it's from our cellar.' He chuckled as if in on some great joke. 'Apparently, it was put there as a decoy, because as you know, churches provided sanctuary to all who asked, people thought there was access to the church…' He now laughed out loud '…while all the time… it was to the house.'

Jenny did her best to look amazed about the tunnels, and

was surprised that the entrance was in the cellar of the Rectory.

'I'd love to see the cellar, it sounds very mysterious'.

Mrs Allen came in with a tea-tray. 'Do you want tea in here, or in the living room?' she asked.

'The living room Jane, if that's ok with you Jenny? So much more comfortable than these hard chairs. I'm just going to show Jenny the cellar, where the tunnel entrance is.'

Jenny stood up and grabbed her coat and followed the Rector back to the kitchen where he opened what looked like a pantry door. Behind it was a stairway which led down to the cellar. They went down the steps. The cellar was empty apart from an old bookcase and it smelt very musty. Jenny could see a wooden door in the wall. 'Is it locked?' she asked.

'No, everybody who knows about the tunnel thinks it goes into the church, so they never bother with it though I don't think the door has been opened in years. It's probably warped.'

They returned upstairs and went to the living room where

Jenny chatted with the Rector and his wife. Jenny had been friends with the Allen's daughter Pippa, until Pippa, aged eighteen, had turned her back on her family and left to live in a kibbutz in Israel. She sent them a card every Christmas to say she was ok, but that was the only communication they ever had from her. They had no idea if she was married, with somebody or even had children. Nobody knew why she went. They continued to chat over tea and biscuits, before Jenny said she ought to go as she'd taken up too much of their time already.

'Tch, Tch, it was lovely to see you my dear, do come again, anytime.' Said Mrs Allen

'Thank you, it was lovely to catch up with you too. Thank you for letting me use the back door, I want to walk back round the churchyard before going home.'

Jenny had been out for the best part of an hour, and needed to walk through the churchyard getting her cheeks cold, to give the impression, she'd been out on a long walk. As she approached the garden gate of Rose Cottage, Jenny could see that the front door was open. She knew she'd shut it on her way out.

'Michael... Michael, the front door's open...' She didn't get any further as a hand clamped over her mouth and she felt something, she presumed was a gun, poke in her back. The front door was then kicked shut by whoever was holding her. She tried to struggle, but her assailant kicked her legs apart, so that if she tried to kick, she would, in all probability, fall over.

'Quiet' a voice hissed 'and stop your squirming it won't do you any good. Now, be a good girl and get yourself in the room down there at the end.'

Jenny moved slowly, and walked to the living room. She was shaking uncontrollably and wasn't sure how she managed to walk. Michael was sat on a kitchen chair with his hands and feet bound with a look on his face that said sorry I didn't mean for this to happen. Two men in balaclavas stood either side of him each holding a gun.

'Sorry Jen…' he started to say

'Shut up' the voice behind her said. She felt sure it was Jim, from the pub.

Jenny looked all about her, as much as she could without turning her head too much. There were just the two men standing by Michael, and a third who still had his hand clamped over her mouth.

Without warning, Jenny was pushed into the sofa. 'Now sit there, like a good girl and do not move, do not speak, and for heaven's sake, do not cry. I hate those girly tears.'

She made herself as comfortable as she could without moving too much. Jenny tried to take in what was happening. Where they really being held hostage in her parent's home? She looked over at Michael.

'Jen, I'm sorry, they burst in…'

Michael was stopped mid-sentence by a well-aimed blow to the cheek with the heel of the gun that the man nearest him, was holding.

'I told you to shut the fuck up. Now I'm sure, she knows you're sorry, but not as sorry as you're gonna be if you don't zip your cakehole.' This was a voice Jenny hadn't heard before.

Jenny had screamed when Michael was struck and found herself with an arm pressing on her windpipe so that she struggled for air.

The other man, shook his head. 'We n-n-need to separate

these t-t-two, or we'll get n-n-nothing done. Put her down in the cellar.'

'Ollie,' Jenny thought.

CHAPTER FIFTEEN

Jenny's attacker removed his arm and pulled her by the hair and told her to stand up. By now the tears that she'd been trying to hold back, were running silently down her face.

'You'd b-b-better let her have the sandwiches that lover-b-b-boy here has so lovingly made her for her lunch' continued Ollie. 'After all, we w-w-wouldn't want the young lady to starve, w-w-would we?'

Jenny was handed a plate of sandwiches from the kitchen, which she almost dropped, and then pushed down the cellar stairs. She managed not to fall and looked about her in case there was somebody else down there. The lights came on as she fell through the doorway.

'Lock that door, I don't want her getting out and messing things up' a muffled voice called out.

Jenny put the plate of sandwiches on the bar and tried to take in what had just happened. Michael was innocent after all. The blow to his face was brutal. These men were Jim and Ollie. Were they the ones he'd been shadowing around Europe? Looking around her, it didn't look like anybody had actually been down here. The two chairs were still against the wall, and she could see the knife on the floor poking out from behind the trunk, where she'd left it. Jenny moved the two chairs to their proper positions around the coffee table, and placed the knife in her pocket where she could feel the newly purchased batteries. She sat down in one of the chairs and tried to make sense of what had just happened. She replaced the batteries in her torch, and put the packaging and old batteries in the bin. She needed to get out of the cellar and get help. She decided to leave the torch and knife by the plate of sandwiches and walked over to the door separating her from Michael, and listened. She could hear what sounded like heavy furniture being moved and shouting, but couldn't hear what was being said. She banged on the door. No response. She banged again and heard someone running down the steps.

'What the fuck do you want?' an angry voice demanded.

'If it's ok with you, I need to go to the bathroom.'

'Wait there, I'll be back in a minute' said the voice.

The man returned a few minutes later.

'Right, straight up, do your business, and straight down. It's no use trying to use the telephone, I've cut the wire. And in case you're thinking of getting your mobile, don't bother, I have it here.' He snarled and held up her phone.

Jenny walked towards the stairs as slowly as she could, wanting to take in the scene of the living room. Michael was sitting slumped in the chair, his chin resting on his chest. A cut on his cheek was dribbling blood. She tried to run over to him, but was stopped short by one of the men in balaclavas standing in front of her and pointing his weapon at her.

'You bastards, what have you done to him?

'Don't ya worry your sweet little head about him, he'll be alright. Now get to the bathroom and be back down here in five minutes, or I'll personally come and shift your backside off the seat.'

Upstairs, Jenny went to her parents' bedroom to use the toilet in their en-suite. She looked around to see if she had anything to use as a weapon, and remembered her mother had a small pistol in her bed-side cabinet. Jenny tip-toed across the floor of her parent's room, quickly found the gun and tucked it in her bra, along with a handful of bullets. It was not very comfortable, but the animals' downstairs were less likely to find it hidden there.

'Your time's up, get your sweet arse down here, or I'm coming up' a voice shouted.

'Alright' she shouted and flushed the toilet.

As she walked through the living room, Jenny could see Michael hadn't moved.

'What do you want, we have nothing of value here?' she demanded.

'It's what he knows, that's what we want?' one of the men in balaclava's replied pointing towards Michael.

'Shut up you fool.' The other man in a balaclava shouted.

'He's just a personal trainer, what use is he to you?'

'Is that what he told you love? Tut, tut, tut. He hasn't been very forthcoming with you has he? Let's hope we have better luck.'

The second man kicked at Michael's chair with such force, causing it to fall over. Michael moaned. Jenny launched herself at the man and found her arms grabbed from behind by the third man before she could do anything.

'Get her back down to the cellar now.' The second man snarled. 'I've had just about enough.'

'Come on, we haven't got all day. If you're a good girl, we'll make you something to eat around six.'

Jenny struggled against her captor but he was too strong for her. He pulled her down the steps and pushed her through the cellar door which he locked behind her. The clock in the living room had read 11.40. It would be just over six hours before they brought her an evening meal. All Jenny could think of was how to get Michael out of there.

She picked at the sandwiches and decided to turn on the jukebox. Fortunately, it was wired so that she didn't have to feed it coins. The juke-box had a volume switch, which Jenny turned down so that it was background music, not that it could be heard upstairs anyway. The intruders obviously didn't know about the access door to the tunnels from the cellar, or they would never have left her down there on her own. They didn't know about the bar either, as she felt sure they would have raided it. She didn't know what the men wanted, but she felt sure it had something to do with her great, great, grandmother's gifts from the Dowager Empress. Jenny needed to find the third package and hide it somewhere they would never find it. She also needed to get help for Michael.

She stuffed the last of the sandwiches in her pocket, then pulled the gun and bullets out from their hiding place in her bra. The chamber held six bullets, two were missing. Giving the gun a quick check over, Jenny placed two bullets in the empty sockets, then put the spares in an inside pocket of her jacket. Having picked up her torch and the knife, she listened at the door that led to the living room. She could hear voices, but nothing more. The jukebox had an option to play any amount of records in a row, by punching in the number and another option that said play all. She pressed the latter and turned the sound up slightly.

She opened both doors to the tunnels, carefully shutting them behind her and made her way down the steps listening out for any voices and footsteps. She paused at the first fork, looking left towards the pub for any signs of movement then carried on to the right. At the next junction, she stopped, looking up at the steps that led to the Rectory. Without hesitation, she climbed the steps to speak to the Rector and his wife about what was happening in the cottage and to call for the police. She tried to open the door, but it wouldn't budge no matter how much she pushed against it. She knew it was useless shouting to the Rector and his wife, they'd never hear her. She turned around feeling defeated and continued down the tunnel turning left towards the Priory. Reaching the steps, Jenny decided to go behind the wall and wait a while. Her legs felt like jelly, her heart like it was running a marathon on its own, and her head not sure what it was doing. She sat down on the floor, switched off her torch and ate the two sandwiches that were now flattened from being pushed in her pocket.

Jenny had decided that if the men were looking for the Russian treasures, it wouldn't be long before they had searched the cottage and would be back at the Priory, either because they had found the letters and clues, or because they had found nothing and this was their remaining option. Ten or fifteen minutes later, she could hear voices. They must have found the key hanging up by the telephone.

'I don't b-b-believe it, n-n-nothing. Are you sure we should have found jewels or something?

It was the voice that belonged to the man called Ollie.

'Yes, I read the letters from her great grandmother.'

This voice was Michael's. This was confusing. She'd just seen him tied up and unconscious on a chair in her parents living room, yet here he was a matter of yards away from her. How could this be?

'The woman wrote home telling her parents all about the wonderful things that the Dowager had given her so there must be items all around the place, but without knowing what we are actually looking for, it is difficult. All we have to go by is a catalogue of items that are listed as missing. Have you looked at that list? It's not as if items have been dispersed around her family, I mean, there's not many of them. Each generation only seems to have produced one child.'

'I'm beginning to think you've led us on a merry dance around Europe and now here, for nothing.'

The voice belonged to the man Jenny didn't know.

'What I've done is taken us on the different journeys made by Tsar Nicholas's mother and his family, to see if we can trace anything. What I do know is that the old woman left Russia with many trunks full of her treasures, yet when she gets back to Denmark, she's got less than half the luggage she set off with. So, you tell me what happened to it.'

'Where's Jim?' the other voice continued.

'Gone back to the pub, he has a business to run. He'll meet us later.' Michael replied

'Ollie, are you sure you searched everywhere in this building? There should be at least three of them priest's holes, and you've only found one under the floorboards.'

'For Pete's sake, Robbie, I searched every fucking square inch of the place. I was going to do another search when that bitch sent me packing, nearly blinding me with her phone. You could always have come and helped me, instead of playing farmer George. Markie, I thought you told her to stay in the house?'

'I did tell her to stay home, and I really wish you wouldn't speak about my wife like that. But then I also gave you lot strict instructions not to contact me, and none of you could do what you were told.'

'Markie's in lurve' Robbie sang.

'Stop calling me Mark, you know I hate that name. Why did I have to be the one called after the family name? It's Michael, M I C H A E L, Michael, got it.'

'Calm down. You're the eldest, so you got the title, or would have done, if it had still been there to inherit. Didn't like the surname either did you Markie? What's wrong with Carruthers, too posh for you? Lord Mark Carruthers, has a certain ring to it, even if there are no lands or money anymore.'

'Michael Black, Ollie, does not draw attention, whereas Michael Carruthers, gets people asking if you're from the posh side of the blanket. You also know full well that in my job I need to be as inconspicuous as I can, not sure Carruthers does that.'

'Yea, I get your point, after all, Michael Carruthers makes you sound like a luvvie, where has Michael Black, dark and mysterious, secret agent…Great acting by the way, even I winced when I thought Jim had pistol-whipped you.'

'For heaven's sake, you two, will you cut it out. We are carrying out the wishes of granny CC, to find the loot that her sister got from Russia, and gain her fair share of it.'

'I still don't understand why or how we're entitled to a share.' Said Robbie.

'I'm beginning to wish we never found those diaries' replied

Michael 'however, finding that missing Faberge Egg is what's driving me on. It must be worth millions if the one found a couple of years ago, is anything to go by. We can all be millionaires, all four of us.'

From where Jenny sat, she could hear the conversations clearly, they must be all stood by the stairs near the trap door. She was shaking with rage. It had all been an act, Michael was not hurt and the bastard was in on it all. She'd been ready to tell him everything, having seen him tied up and beaten, but that son-of-a-bitch was not going to get his hands on anything, if she could help it. She tried to remember where she'd heard the name Carruthers before, but her brain wouldn't release the information. The other questions now circling her brain were who was granny CC and what diaries. He'd also lied about his name, unless of course, he'd changed it by deed-poll.

'Right' said Michael 'let's all three of us go up to the very top and scour every inch of this place. We'll work our way down, and for once, we will work together. We'll meet Jim back at the cottage around 6pm. He said he'll feed us all with pub grub.'

Jenny waited about five minutes before venturing out from

her hiding place having heard three sets of feet stomp their way up the stairs. Cautiously, she went up the steps and gently pushed the trap door. Fortunately, it was not bolted and she lifted it enough to be able to see around the floor area. Scanning round as far as she could, she saw all was clear. She pushed the door open to its fullest extent, climbed out and put the door back into position. While still checking all around her, she tip-toed her way over to the linen cupboard and opened the doors and tried to lift up the base of the cupboard. She just couldn't get her fingernails in deep enough to lift it. She put her hands in her pockets while thinking what to do and felt the knife, that should do the trick.

Jenny stuck the knife in between the shelf and the frame and managed to lever the base up and peered in. She could see that the base board was counter-levered from the back of the cupboard. Clever. Had her arms been long enough, she would have been able to press down at the back of the cupboard and the shelf should have lifted up. The underside of the base had a knob, presumably to close it down once the priest had got inside. She tried to imagine what the scenario would have been. Those hiding would have clambered in, the shelf put back down in place and linen put back in the cupboard. Most of the linen, she guessed, would have been placed at the front of the cupboard so as not to interfere with the balancing system.

Jenny didn't have to imagine it for long, she could hear a set of feet coming down the stairs from the attic. She couldn't run back to the trapdoor without being seen from the stairs. There was nothing for it, she heaved herself up into the cupboard and pulled the two doors shut behind her. The space behind the drawers was roomy, and she pulled the base shelf down just as she heard the footsteps on the lower staircase.

'Ollie, what you doing down there? Get your arse back up here now and pull your weight.'

'Hold your horses M-m-markie, I only came down for me hat, it's bloody f-f-freezing in that attic. I'm coming right back up.'

His hat was on the floor at the base of the newel post at the bottom of the stairs. As he picked it up, Ollie noticed that the door was open that hid the trap-door. He walked round to it, looked inside, bolted the trap door and shut the hidden door in the panelling.

Jenny waited for the foot-steps to climb back up before

switching on her torch. The torchlight showed that there was space enough for two people to sit facing each other with the possibility of another crouched on the floor. A small bench had been built into the two ends to act as seats. She managed to kneel on the floor and look under each seat where she found nothing but cobwebs. Shining the torch above her head, Jenny could see that the base could be held in place with three flat pegs that spun around into a groove where the top of the drawers would be. This house was full of surprises, so it didn't seem odd that she started pressing the perimeter of her den. On the back wall, a square of the panelling moved slightly. Jenny tried pressing in the corners, and along the edges, but it didn't spring open. What it did do, was slide. Her fingers were cold and slippery and she couldn't get much purchase on it, so she licked her fingers, rubbed them together and managed to move the panel. The torchlight showed her a familiar polythene wrapped package. It wasn't large, just the size of a tissue box. She slipped the package inside her jacket, and pulled the panel shut as far as she could. The last half inch wouldn't close and try as she might, she could not get the panel to shift. It would have to stay like that.

Jenny switched off her torch and raised the bottom shelf, listening to what was going on in the rest of the house.

There was a lot of stomping about in the upper parts of the house and a lot of moaning about how cold it was. She pushed the doors open and scrambled out, pushing the secret compartment base closed and shutting the doors. She thought about leaving the priory through the front door, but realised that it would only need one of them to be looking out of a window and see her, which would give the game up.

She tip-toed back across the hall to the panelled wall and counted the panels to find the one that opened the door. Unbolting the trap door, she opened it, and shut the panelled door behind her. As she pulled the trap door down, it thudded into place. Jenny stood still in horror, in case it had been heard upstairs. There was nothing for it, she needed to get away from this part of the tunnel as quickly as she could. She willed her feet into action. They felt like they were encased in cement, but she managed to make them move. Breaking into a run, Jenny looked behind her to see if she was being followed. At each fork, she stopped briefly and checked for any sounds. It was only when she reached the steps to Rose Cottage cellar, that she could hear someone moving. She raced up the steps, the door wouldn't open.

'Oh, don't be so stupid, open up' she commanded the door latch 'I'm in danger of being caught and I value my life, so please be a good door latch and open.'

It finally opened and she pushed open the inner door. Closing the outer door behind her, Jenny took the knife from her pocket and wedged it into the latch mechanism then pushed the inner door shut. She wasn't sure where to hide the package. Looking about her, she saw the trunk, the lounge chairs and the jukebox. She ruled out the trunk, that would be the first place they'd look. She thought about the fridge, but that would be too obvious. She inspected the lounge chairs and found that the padded seat lifted up. She went over to the jukebox and tried to move it away from the wall. It moved slightly, but was far too heavy for her to move any further. She lifted up the seat cushion and managed to place the package in the space. The seat fell back into place without any effort.

Jenny sat down, trying to get her breathing under control. There was no difference in the comfort of the seat, so hopefully it would serve as a safe place. She took off her coat, and tucked the pistol into her jeans pocket, ensuring the safety was on. She wandered over to the bar and poured herself a few fingers of whisky. Jenny sat back down and took a couple of generous sips of her drink and waited for six o'clock to arrive. A little before six o'clock, Jenny heard the key turn in the lock and the door open. Michael limped in, a black bruise under his left eye and a plaster on his cheek.

'O God, Jen, you're ok. I've been so worried about you. They've gone. Couldn't find what they wanted or thought they'd find. It's safe now. Come on upstairs and I'll make you a hot drink.'

'How did you get free?'

'They must have knocked me out, I came too and found they'd cut the ties on my wrists and ankles and nobody there.'

Jenny looked at him in horror, who was he kidding, she knew all about his game now, but decided to play along.

'Don't worry about the face, I'm used to it' he said. 'It'll turn a lovely shade of purple then yellow. It's you I'm worried about. Did they hurt you?'

He thought the look of horror was to do with his face, 'the self-effacing bastard,' she thought to herself.

'No, no they didn't hurt me, in fact they were quite good. Even let me go to the loo – but you'd been knocked out at the point. What did they want?

'I'm not sure love, but let's get you back upstairs.'

Jenny was feeling scared of being left alone with Michael. What if he turned on her?

Michael made his way over to the jukebox. 'How do you stop all this music?'

'Press the button that says stop' Jenny replied glibly as she grabbed her jacket and walked out of the cellar to the living room. She looked around her. Nothing much seemed to have been moved or displaced and a quick glance in her mother's glass cabinet showed the items Jenny had stowed there to be still in place.

'I hope you don't mind, but I thought we'd grab some food from the pub.'

'Shouldn't we call the police. I mean you've been tied up and attacked, I've been scared witless and heaven only knows if anything's missing.'

'I don't think they were after anything from the house love, it was information I might have had they were after. It appears I didn't know what they wanted, so they've gone.'

'But…'

'Jen, it was work related so informing the Police is futile.'

Jenny couldn't believe that he wanted to go out to the pub after everything they'd been through.

'Not sure I really want to go out, Michael. She certainly didn't want to chance seeing Jim. Is there nothing in the fridge?

'How about I ring the pub and ask for a delivery?'

'I didn't know they did that.'

'They probably don't, but there's no harm in asking is there?'

Jenny went to the kitchen and opened the fridge and having inspected the contents before walking back to the doorway.

'I'd be quite happy with a baked potato, sausages and baked beans.'

'Ok that'll be fine, do you want me to cook it?' Michael said wincing as he got up.

'No, you sit down and make yourself as comfortable as you can, those thugs obviously beat you up a bit.'

Jenny turned her head so that Michael couldn't see the tears that were running down her cheeks. How could he lie to her like that? Picking up two large potatoes, she stabbed them with a fork, imagining them to be Michael, or one of the assailants. She cooked them in the microwave for five minutes before placing them in the oven so that the skins would firm up, then cooked the sausages. She heard Michael enter the kitchen and open the fridge door then the pop of a bottle of prosecco. He came up behind her and slipped one arm around her waist and nestled his head into her neck, while offering her one of the two glasses he held in the other hand. Jenny took a deep breath in, thanking God that she had put her mother's gun back in her coat pocket.

'Let's celebrate our new-found freedom' he said, 'and release from captivity.'

Jenny cried louder.

'There, there love, it's alright now, we're safe. They've

gone.'

If only he knew what she was really feeling. She wanted to smash the bottle over his head and tell him she knew what a lying conniving son of a bitch he was.

'So what happened?' Jenny asked. 'I go out for a walk, and you get attacked!'

'Well, I saw you go out, then I thought I'd surprise you with lunch for when you got back. I was in the kitchen making us sandwiches, when there was a knock on the door. As I opened it, I was knocked to the ground. I banged my head and must have lost consciousness, cos when I opened my eyes, I was tied to the kitchen chair with those bloody plastic ties. I tried asking what they wanted, but they didn't say anything.'

What he didn't tell her was that as soon as she'd left the cottage, Ollie, Jim and Robbie had come in through the back door. Ollie had applied theatrical make up to Michael's face, while Jim had prepared the sandwiches. Robbie had tied Michael to the stool, very enthusiastically and they waited for Jenny to return. They just wanted her down in the cellar, so that they knew where she was.

'Where they that dissident group you were telling me about that you were following round Europe?'

'I'm pretty sure they were, but I couldn't swear to it. They spent ten minutes pacing round the chair, not saying anything, just staring at me. Then they started with the questioning.'

'Like what?'

'It was proper interrogation, you don't need to know, it will only upset you. They'd just decided that they needed to search the house when you came in. I tried to warn you, but they threatened they'd kill you if I called out. I'm sorry Jen if I've dragged you into my work.'

Michael managed to shed some tears which Jenny wasn't sure were real or forced.

They ate their dinner in relative silence. Jenny was hesitant in speaking to Michael at all, in case she said the wrong thing. Having eaten half of her meal, she pushed the plate away. She hadn't touched her drink.

'I guess I wasn't that hungry after all. I've got a migraine coming on, I think I'll go to bed and hopefully sleep it off.

I'm glad you're ok.'

'I'm not surprised, it's been one hell of a day. You go to bed love, I'll sleep in the spare room so as not to disturb you.'

She got up from the table, said good night, kissed Michael on the cheek causing him to wince, and went upstairs to bed. As she walked across the landing from the bathroom, Jenny could hear Michael talking on his mobile.

'She seems ok… no, it can't have been Jenny in the tunnel. Have you seen the walls in the cellar, they are covered in tongue and groove all the fucking way round. No doors, no niches, no nothing, just the one door in and out which you locked. It looks like she drank scotch all afternoon listening to the jukebox. No bloody wonder she's gone to bed with a bloody migraine… How the hell do I know how a bar of chocolate from the local shop got down there perhaps Robbie or Jim dropped it?'

Jenny gasped, her bar of chocolate, it must have fallen out of her pocket.

'Yes it's her favourite chocolate, but I'm telling you, unless she can now perform magic and transport herself, it wasn't Jenny… What do you mean you bolted the trap door, then found it unbolted? It could only be done from inside the place, and there were only the three of us in there… no you're mistaken, you obviously didn't draw the bolt in the first place… I'll see you in the morning, I'll go for a run, usual place.'

The turmoil Jenny had felt just over a year ago, when Michael first went missing, had returned like a bowling ball aimed at her head. She cried herself to sleep and hoped that when she did wake in the morning, she'd find it had all been a dream.

Making her way downstairs, the next morning, Jenny found a note propped against the kettle.

Gone for a run, to blew the cobwebs. Back later. xx

'How the bloody hell can you go out for a run.' She shouted at the note. 'You're covered in bruises and you were limping.' Was his whole life a lie?

Jenny got herself a coffee and toast and sat down at the kitchen table, wondering what to do next. She knew, resolutely, she couldn't tell Michael anything. She no longer trusted him at all and was glad she'd made the decision to hide all the papers she'd found from her grandparents.

'Blowing the cobwebs away is a good idea.' She said to herself, and got herself ready for a walk, fetching her wallet from her bag and ensuring she had her mother's gun, before leaving. She walked to the shops opposite the pub and went inside.

'I know this might sound like a daft question but do you sell pay as you go mobile phones?'

'Yes, as a matter of fact we do, they've been one of our best sellers in the last few weeks. Do you need a sim card as well?'

'Yes please, can you top it up with thirty pounds? Thanks'

'You'll find it's ready charged too.'

'That's very good service.'

'Not one we were doing until a couple of weeks ago when we had two different people come in asking if we could charge it for them.'

A village shop seemed a strange place to have mobile phones as their best seller, Jenny thought, but then she was doing exactly that, buying a phone. Jenny handed over her debit card and paid the bill. She decided to walk back to the cottage, the long way round, just as she'd done at Christmas. On her way, she tried calling her parents. Receiving no answer, she texted them.

Hope you're both still having a great time. Staying here for another week. Can you remind me of the surname of the new tenant at the farm? If you don't recognise the number, I misplaced my phone, so bought a cheap replacement. Lots of love Jen xx

As Jenny rounded the corner at the bottom of Church Hill, she noticed what looked like a motorbike outside the cottage. Nearing the cottage gate, she saw that the front door was wide open. Talk about déjà vu. Heedful of the previous day's events, Jenny reached for her mother's gun in her coat pocket and firmly in hand, released the safety catch and put her hand back in her pocket. As she approached the front door, two men in black leather and motor cycle helmets came running out with a large rucksack. Neither seemed alarmed or surprised to see Jenny stood at the doorway. They both sported guns and aimed at Jenny.

'Don't move' shouted the first man.

She thought it was Michael, but the voice was slightly muffled from the bike helmet and the visor was down, so she couldn't see his face. Jenny stood rooted to the spot, she felt that couldn't have moved even if her life depended on it.

As they ran past her, one of them fired at her, and missed. Jenny, having pulled her hand out of her pocket, automatically fired back, hitting one of them, but couldn't determine which one she'd hit or where she'd hit them. To Jenny it felt like everyone was moving in slow motion, even as the two men made it to the bike and sped away. The sound of gun fire brought a couple of neighbours out of their homes. Jenny dropped the gun and sank to the floor shaking. She felt dizzy, the world was spinning round her in a blur.

'Jenny, are you ok? Are you hurt?' It was Mrs Allen. She sounded like she was talking under water.

'Jenny, are you ok?' she repeated.

Dazed, Jenny replied 'I'm ok… they missed…' She started to cry.

'Tch tch dear, it'll all be alright. Derek's just gone inside to see what's going on in there.'

Jenny saw the Rector come back out of the cottage.

'There's nobody in there, but the place is a bit of a mess I'm afraid.'

'I need to see. O God, this can't be happening.' Jenny was confused and in shock. Yesterday three thugs had tied up Michael and held her hostage in the cellar, and now two people had been in the cottage ransacking the place. Was it the same people or an incredible coincidence?

She stood up uneasily and made her way inside the cottage with Mrs Allen, and Mrs Robbins from next door. The Rector dashed across the road to the vicarage.

'Oh my god, look at all this mess.'

The bookshelf had been emptied, the books lying where they'd been thrown. Pictures had been torn from the walls and furniture upturned with cushions thrown about like Frisbees. Remarkably the glass cabinet was intact.

'Tch tch dear, this will soon get cleared up, and for heaven's sake call me Jane. By the time we've cleared this mess up, you'll hardly notice the difference.'

Mrs Robbins set to in the kitchen making a pot of tea. The

rector returned from the vicarage having phoned for the police.

'The police are on their way and say not to touch anything. Their forensics team will also be here in a jiffy.'

Jenny stood in a trance muttering to herself.

'I don't believe it, this is bizarre, what did they want?'

She noticed her notepad on which she'd written down the clues her grandparents had left her, lying on the floor. The page was missing. Whoever had caused all of this chaos, must have found it, but was that yesterday or today?

Jenny ran down the steps to the cellar. The contents of the trunk had been emptied onto the floor, the jukebox had been pulled away from the wall, and the lounge chairs were lying on their side with all the seat cushions removed. The third package she'd retrieved only the day before was missing.

'Noooooo, the bastards, finally got what they were looking for.'

She ran back to the living room and searched through the glass cabinet. The egg cups, coffee spoons and cruet set were still in place.

'Excuse me Jane, I just need to check upstairs.' Jenny ran upstairs to her bedroom and checked the hiding place in the rafter. It had not been disturbed, neither had her jewellery box. She made her way back downstairs to the kitchen where she sat down and given a strong cup of tea that must have had at least five spoonsful of sugar in it. She pulled a face.

'God that's sweet'

'For the shock' she was told.

The police arrived ten minutes later and asked Jenny if there was anything missing. How was she going to explain about the Faberge Egg? Mrs Robbins said she'd pop back home and was happy to come back to help clear up when needed.

'Mrs Black, I'm Detective Inspector Barnes and this is Officer Dana Arnold who also works as a Victim Support Officer. Now we realise this must be all a bit of a shock for you, and we'll be helping you all along the way. Do you know if there is anything missing at all?

The Inspector looked to be about forty years of age and

although dressed in a suit, looked like he would have been more comfortable in jeans and sweatshirt. Dana, was about Jenny's age, dark haired and was comfortably dressed in jeans and blouse. The appearance of the police officers seemed to reawaken Jenny. Whoever had done this was not going to get away with it.

'Yes, part of my twenty-first birthday present from my grandparents… I only found it yesterday…'

She went on to explain how that her grandparents had both died before her birthday, but had left her clues for a treasure hunt, which she'd only found a few days ago. Both police officers listened intently, as did the Rector and his wife.

'Can you describe the items that have been taken?' DI Barnes asked.

'I can tell you what they were, but not a description. There were two items, as far as I'm aware'

'As far as you're aware?'

'Yes, from the letters and clues, there would have been a small gold plate and a Faberge Egg. I didn't get to open the package before I hid it.'

There was an audible gasp from Jane Allen. 'A Faberge egg as in the Russian eggs?

'Yes.'

'Why did you have to hide it?' Dana asked gently.

'It's a long story' said Jenny and continued to tell them everything including the events of the previous day.

'Why didn't you report this yesterday?' Dana enquired.

'I wanted to, but Michael, said it would be useless, that nothing could be done. He said it was all to do with him and his work.'

'Tch Tch dear, why on earth didn't you tell us Michael was back yesterday morning when you visited?

'Please don't take this the wrong way, but I didn't know who to trust… I tried to get help from you, but your cellar door wouldn't budge, I couldn't open it.'

'Your neighbours here heard gunshots.'

'Yes, the two men, they both had guns. One of them fired

at me and I shot back.'

'Where is the gun you used?'

Jenny looked down at her hands. 'Um I don't know, I must have dropped it.'

'Would this be it?' DI Barnes held out the gun which was in a plastic bag.

'Yes, that's it, I think.'

'Does it belong to you?'

'No, it's my mothers.'

'Do you have a licence to fire this?'

'No, no I don't.'

'But you did use it.'

'Yes'

'Why?'

'I've just told you. It was self-defence, one of those bastards shot at me, and missed, I just automatically fired back. I think I hit one of them, but I'm not sure.'

'Ok, Mrs Black, I have all that written down. Please could you read through it and if you agree with what is written, sign it here at the bottom.'

Jenny read the statement through a haze of tears and signed it.

'Now would you like Dana to stay with you?'

'Tch Tch, don't worry about Jenny, Mr Barnes, I'll stay with her, Derek and I will make sure she's ok. Can we tidy up now?'

'Thank-you Mrs Allen, when my team have finished their work, then you can tidy up. We need to see if we can find any fingerprints.'

'Oh God,' exclaimed Jenny, 'Michael was out for a run, he hasn't come back yet.'

She was interrupted by one of the Forensics Team. 'DI Barnes, could I have a quick word with you please. We found this upstairs.'

'Mrs Black, there is an envelope here, with your name on it.

Would you care to open it please?'

Jenny's hands shook as she opened the envelope and read the message inside.

Jen, I'm sorry to have caused you all this heartache, and mess. I did fall in love with you, and if I could have done things differently, I would have. Sorry. M.

She just sat shaking her head in disbelief, tears clouding her vision. And crumpled the paper in her fist. Dana took the paper out of her hands and handed it to DI Barnes who excused himself from the room for a few minutes.

Jenny spoke to Dana. 'Michael had a red fiat in the pub car park. I don't know if it's still there or not...'

'We'll check.'

Jenny's mobile phone beeped to announce the arrival of a text message. It was from her parents.

Still having a super time, moving into the mountains later today. Name of tenant is Robert Carruthers. See you soon Mum and Dad xx

DI Barnes came back. 'I've put out a warrant for Jim

Redcar, Landlord of the pub.'

'Perhaps you'd better also go round to the farm and arrest the farmer. His name is Robert Carruthers, and while you're at it, Michael, who is actually Mark Carruthers also known as Simon Pellham and, there's someone called Oliver. I've been well and truly used in their game.'

'Did you know any of them, apart from Michael?' DI Barnes asked.

'No. Well I'd seen Jim in the pub, and I recall seeing Ollie or Oliver at the library once. But other than that, no.'

Jane sat down next to Jenny with a handful of tissues which she pressed into Jenny's hand.

'Thank-you Mrs Black, you've been most helpful. I am sorry for all this. I will keep in touch with you and let you know how we're getting on and of course you can contact Dana any time you want. We may have further questions which we will need to ask you. I don't hold out much luck on retrieving your lost items. I'm sure you're aware that Faberge Eggs are very much sought after and will go to the highest bidder once it's known it's available. Unless of course, we can intercept it.'

'Thank-you Mr Barnes, you've been very helpful. Thank-you Dana. Please excuse me if I don't get up, I'm not sure my legs would hold me right at this moment.'

The Forensics team left not long after the Detective, leaving Jenny in the company of Jane.

'Jane, do you mind very much, if we tidy these things away now. I can't stand looking at the mess.'

'Tch Tch of course, my dear.'

Jenny tried to stand, her legs buckling underneath her.

'Tch, Tch, just sit there a while, you've had a big shock. We'll sort this out in a few minutes.'

Jane Allen set to work picking up books and papers off the floor, righting chairs and rehanging pictures. There were a couple of broken glasses, but other than that, damage had been kept very much to a minimum.

'Thank-you Jane, I feel so lazy letting you do all the work.'

'It's not a problem. Now, do you want to come and stay at the Rectory, you'd be more than welcome?'

'Thank-you Jane, for the offer, but I'll stay here. Whoever they were, they got what they came for, they won't be back.'

'Ok, now I'll be back in a jiffy with a meal for you. I have a casserole in the oven.'

'I'll be alright, I don't want to deprive you of your casserole.'

'Tch Tch, I always cook more than we can eat, we have plenty.'

Jenny turned on the one o'clock news, mainly to hear what had been going on in the world apart from her own tragedy. The local news followed, with no mention of anything that had been going on in the village that morning which filled her with slight relief. Later that afternoon, DI Barnes and Dana returned.

'We've arrested both Jim and Robert at the farm. They are apparently brothers.' DI Barnes explained.

'Are you sure, Jim has a different surname' Jenny told them.

'Yes, when questioned, he said it was an amalgamation of surnames from his family. Whatever that means. It would appear that they have been using the tunnels between the pub and the farm for smuggling purposes. Counterfeit drink would be delivered to the farm, then the pair of them would move it to the pub via the tunnel. A pair of racketeers is how I think one would describe them. The one called Robert, isn't very bright. When asked if he had anything else to say, he said no, but we'd never find their brothers Oliver and Mark. So, he has confirmed that there are four of them, without me doing much spade work.'

Jenny tried to process the fact that Michael was possibly called Mark and wasn't an only child, that he actually had three brothers.

CHAPTER SIXTEEN

Jenny woke feeling like some great burden had been lifted from her. Perhaps she'd finally shifted Michael from her life. Strange how a couple of weeks can change one's perspective on someone; from pining for them to return, to glad to be rid of them. She'd checked under the bed the night before to see if Michael's bag was still there and was relieved to see it gone. As she stepped out onto the landing in the morning, she checked the spare room where Michael had slept on his own the night before last. Poking out from under the covers was a computer bag which on investigation held his laptop and his wedding ring.

'That's it then, he's definitely gone this time if he's left his ring. Obviously doesn't mean that much to him.'

She looked down at her own ring and twisted it off her finger. She placed both rings on the bedside cabinet in her room. As Jenny reached the bottom stair, she noticed suitcases in the hall, and the unmistakable aroma of bacon being cooked.

'Michael?' she called out.

There was no answer, she entered the kitchen cautiously

where she was relieved to find her parents.

'What are you doing here?' she asked.

'Well love, it is our home' her father replied.

'I mean, what are you doing here now, you were going onto part two of your holiday yesterday.'

'Derek and Jane called us' replied her mother 'they were very concerned about you, and quite rightly. We couldn't leave you on your own to sort this out, so here we are. We managed to get seats on last night's flight.'

'Why didn't you tell us Michael was alive and had come back?'

'I wasn't sure myself, how I felt about it. He acted like he'd only been away for a couple of days or weeks, couldn't really see the hurt he'd caused me. It seemed that as he'd been in touch with me throughout the year posing as a friend, so perhaps in his eyes, everything was ok. I think that all he was interested in was the family heirlooms. Jenny collapsed onto a kitchen chair. 'I'm so glad you're here. I feel sort of guilty for not wanting Michael in my life anymore. There's such a lot to tell you.'

'How about we have breakfast,' interjected her father 'and then you can tell us what happened.'

The radio was on in the background and they all heard the news as it came on.

'A man's body has been found on the M6, south of Birmingham. It is thought he was a pillion passenger on a motor cycle. The man has yet to be identified. Police are appealing for witnesses who may have seen the incident to come forward or ring the incident room. In other news, an attempted robbery in Wartlington was thwarted yesterday, when a bird-scarer fired and scared off the would-be robbers. The weather for today…'

'Oh…' Jenny went very pale, the fork she was holding clattered onto the plate 'do you think the man's body is one of the men I shot yesterday? What if I've killed him? What if…'

'Well love, if it is, the police will be in contact. Try not to worry too much.'

'Of course, Dad, you're right. But… what if it is one of them, and he's died because I shot him, I'll be arrested for murder. What if it was Michael?'

Jenny covered her face with her hands hoping it would blot out the scenario that was playing in her head of Michael on the back of a motorcycle, her shooting him and him falling off it in the middle of a stream of traffic.

'You mustn't upset yourself. Remember one of them fired at you and you fired back, just like anyone would do, in the circumstances...' Jenny's father looked at her mother.

'I'm not sure it works quite like that, especially if you shot in self-defence. Like your dad says, try not to worry too much, we'll sort it out.'

Jenny's parents tried to deflect her thoughts.

'How about after breakfast, you show us all the papers? I remember your grandparents planning something for your twenty-first birthday, but they never let on, even to us, what it was. Did you know that they used to call you little wren?' her mother asked

'No, why?'

'It was when you were born, the first girl born in the family for generations; and they knew we'd hand on the wren salt at your baptism, and because you were Jenny...'

'I was a little Jenny wren' she laughed 'how sweet.'

Jenny told her parents all about the tunnels and finding the gifts that her grandparents had hidden for her.

'I'd forgotten about the door in the panelling downstairs,' said her father, 'I'm not sure I can remember the exact place, I did such a great job getting it to blend in.'

'You certainly did do a good job, I stomped around for ages on the floor before I wondered if it was hidden in the wall. Did you ever go down into the tunnels dad?'

'Yes, it was as good as a playground for me, when I was growing up, for me and my playmates. Hide and seek was a great game to play down there.'

'What about the items you found, Jenny, where are they?' her mother asked.

'Well three lots are hidden in your cabinet over there, see if you can spot them while I fetch some items from upstairs.'

Jenny's mother spent a good few minutes surveying the shelves of her cabinet, before reaching in and bringing out the cruet set and the egg cups.

'Well I never, it looks like they've always been in there. I can't see a third lot though. Just look at this egg cup Philip. I can't tell if it's gold or silver lined with gold...'

'Coffee spoons' was all Jenny said.

Her mother went back to the cabinet and searched.

'My word, they are beautiful, look at this enamelling.'

Jenny showed them the sapphire and pearl necklace, placing it around her mother's neck.

'Exquisite' her father exclaimed, bowing to his wife 'not that you could wear it out in public without an armed guard though.'

Jenny's parents were as equally amazed at the crimson leather box and the papers it had contained.

'There's something else in the cellar, I'll be right back.' Jenny returned wearing the tiara.

'Goodness me, that is beautiful.' Exclaimed her mother 'I wonder what made the Empress think Genevieve would be able to wear it?'

'Well you've certainly had an adventure,' remarked her father 'you need to show me the priests' holes, I've never actually seen them.'

'They're amazing. While I was there I made a note of some work that needs doing. There's water getting in, in the attic, and the floorboards are now rotten.'

'Thanks love, I'll get that sorted.'

DI Barnes and Dana arrived while Jenny was telling her father that she needed to replace some of his bottles from the cellar.

'Mrs Black...' started DI Barnes

'Please call me Jenny, I've never gone by Mrs Black, I kept my maiden name when I got married.'

'Jenny,' carried on the detective, 'I don't know if you've heard the news today, but a man's body has been found.'

Jenny paled and sat down.

'Yes, it was on the radio while we were having breakfast.'

'We have reason to believe that it is your husband, Michael.'

Jenny gasped, the colour drained out of her. 'Oh my God, I killed him...'

Panic overwhelmed her as she listened to the officers. She would go to prison for this. Killing someone even in self-defence was a punishable offence.

'Now, now, we're not sure that the bullet you shot, did hit him. All we know is we have a body of a man in motorcycle leathers. We do, however, need you to come and identify the body...' he hesitated 'I'm afraid there is a lot of damage to the body, so it may not be easy. We can always try and get dental records...'

CHAPTER SEVENTEEN

The thought of looking at Michael, dead, filled her with horror.

'Does it have to be me?' she whispered.

'You are his next of kin, if it is Michael. I totally understand how hard this is…'

'Ok, when? I'm not sure I'm ready for this. Can we do it now, if I have to sit and wait, I'm not sure I'll be able to do it at all.'

'Yes of course,' Dana replied gently 'your parents are welcome to accompany you if you wish.'

Jenny's mother put a protective arm around her and spoke soothingly to her, like she had when Jenny was a little girl and had woken up with bad dreams.

'Come on love, we'll do this together, it will be alright.'

The mortuary was a grey-white stone building, void of any colour. It was edged on one side by a bank of trees, which in the summer probably brought life to the building, but here, in the middle of winter, it was drab and sad. There were no flower borders, just grass. The doors into the building were tinted smoky grey and opened automatically as they were approached. The corridors were well lit and void of any decoration. The waiting room they had been shown to wasn't much better. Black leather, steel framed chairs lined the walls. The only other furniture was a matching coffee table with a box of tissues set on top. Jenny and her parents spoke in hushed tones, as if, speaking normally would have been offensive to the mortuary occupants. Dana sat with Jenny trying to offer her support, stroking her hand. The door opposite to the one they had entered through, opened. DI Barnes came through it with another gentleman dressed in dark grey striped trousers, black jacket, white shirt and black tie. Both wore a sombre look on their faces.

'Jenny, you may come through, when you're ready.' DI Barnes spoke softly. 'All I need you to do is to say whether you believe the deceased is Michael or not.'

'Mum, will you come with me, I don't think I can do this on my own? I can't stop shaking.'

'Of course, love. Just take your time. Take a few deep breaths and when you're ready, we'll go through.'

Jenny took a few deep breaths as suggested by her mother. She wasn't sure she could get her heart rate any steadier, so stood up, 'Ok, I'm ready.' She walked through the open door with her mother just behind her. The body was on a trolley, with a sheet covering it, turned down neatly at the neck. She could see the head and face clearly and studied it. It was badly bruised and swollen, making it difficult for a clear identification. The height was about right, and the physical build. The hair was still covered in blood, so it was hard to distinguish the colour.

'I'm pretty sure it's Michael' Jenny whispered.

'Thank-you Jenny. We have checked the finger prints, and they match those we found in the cottage on items Michael touched. We're also confident, that this is Michael.'

Jenny stared at the face trying to see through the bruising and swelling. She turned and left the room before dissolving into tears in her father's arms.

Jenny had wanted to show her father the tunnels, but the Police advised that they were still part of their investigations and were out of bounds for the foreseeable future, as was the Priory. Her father served notice on the farm tenant, Robert Carruthers, whether he was guilty or not of any crime, he didn't want the man anywhere near the family home. The farm labourers were happy to continue running the farm. It appeared that Robert hadn't done any hands-on work from the day he took over the tenancy. One of the workers told Philip that he would be interested in taking over the tenancy, and they agreed to a three-month probation period. Though Philip suspected that it wouldn't be needed, the man worked hard and had kept the farm running since the first tenant left.

Jenny rang the library and spoke to Kate.

'Hi Kate, I thought I ought to let you know that Michael's body has been found.'

'Oh God, Jenny, that's awful. How are you feeling... no scrap that, you're obviously feeling terrible.'

'I'm ok, I'm with my parents. I just wanted to let you know, because I don't know when I'll be back, or even if I want to come back.'

'Take your time, Jenny. I'll put you on compassionate leave and when you feel able, come in for a chat.'

'Thanks Kate, you've been really patient with me.'

244

'Not at all, I don't know how you've coped with any of this. Just take your time and I'll see you soon.'

A week after their visit to the mortuary, DI Barnes and Dana visited Jenny at her parents' home.

'In my little chats with Robert Carruthers, I've learned a lot about family history.' DI Barnes told her. 'It would appear that you are related to the Carruthers brothers through both sides of your parents' families.'

Jenny looked puzzled. 'Wouldn't that make my marriage to Michael void? In fact, is my marriage legal? Shouldn't I be Mrs Carruthers?'

'That's something we will have to investigate. However, it appears that both of your parents have a great grandmother who were sisters.'

The detective referred to his notes. 'Genevieve Rosseau and Cecile Rosseau.'

'Yes, we know a little about them. Genevieve worked in service as maid to the Dowager Empress of Russia, and Cecile married into the landed gentry here in the UK.' Jenny informed him.

'Err yes, that's what I have here.' DI Barnes tapped his notebook. 'Apparently Lord Carruthers, Cecile's father-in-law, spent all the family money gambling. Even sold objects from the house to pay his debts. By the time Mark Carruthers, Cecile's husband, came to inherit the title, there was nothing left, not even the grand house. Robert Carruthers told me that Cecile wrote diaries which tell of her life from when she was first courted by Mark Carruthers. It seems that he spotted her on the boat from France to England and asked her about her trip. Being young and naïve, she told him all about her sister. I guess he saw her as an answer to some of the family's problems, so courted and married her very quickly.'

'A cash cow, poor Cecile.'

'Yes, I suppose so. He pushed her to ask her sister for financial help or for the odd trinket, but was turned down by Genevieve telling her that anything she had been given was obviously of little value.'

'That would be because Genevieve didn't know that she'd been given or left things by the Dowager for many years. I have a letter she wrote to my grandfather that says she only discovered them when they moved out of the farm to Rose

Cottage.' Jenny interrupted.

'Further diary entries show that many requests for help were made and each turned down. It would seem that each successive generation of the Carruthers family have blamed Genevieve for their demise from the high standing in society they had enjoyed, and these four brothers, having learned about the Romanov family and the connections of their great, great aunt, decided it was time to redress the balance.'

'Mum, did you know anything about this?'

'No, I didn't realise that Carruthers was a family name. As you know I haven't yet investigated any of my side of the family. My family are all Graham's. It's a bit of shock to think we're related to people who think everyone owes them a living.'

'Mrs Bird, I'm not surprised you don't know anything about this branch of your family. Cecile and Mark Carruthers had seven children, something like three boys and four girls. My guess is, that as they married and branched out, so to speak, your family tree grew quite wide.'

'Have you found Oliver yet?' Jenny enquired.

'No, not yet. He's probably gone into hiding, but he'll want to sell his booty before too long. We have reason to believe that he will be selling other items he has procured, with your items, at the same time. This will, at the same time, draw out other leeches in the system, hopefully. There is a big, big market for Romanov treasures and other items associated with the family. We are working with Interpol and MI6.'

'I had no idea. Michael said he was working with MI5/MI6, or something like that. I wonder if Michael made the connection between our families before we were married or when I found that letter from Genevieve's parents?'

'Yes he was, but he seems to have turned his work to his advantage and that of his brothers. On the subject of Michael, I can confirm that the bullet that hit him, is the one that killed him…'

Jenny gasped.

'Jenny, it was not fired from your weapon. It is possible, that Oliver killed him so that he could keep the goods for himself, or Michael was a threat in turning his brother in. We may never know.'

Relief flooded through Jenny. She hadn't killed him after all. She must have missed when she fired the weapon.'

'You mean there is a possibility that Michael was innocent in all this? Jenny's mother asked.

'No, not at all. He was not an innocent party. In security terms, I guess you could say he turned rogue. Knowing that it wasn't you Jenny, who killed Michael, we can now allow you to hold a funeral. The body will be released. I have here the personal effects from Michael, his watch, wedding ring and money.' He handed over a small self-seal poly bag. 'With regard to your missing items...'

'Would it help to have photographs of all the items?' Jenny's mum asked.

Jenny frowned, puzzled. 'I never got round to taking photographs of the plate and the egg. I only have a description.'

'You're forgetting what a resourceful grandmother you had. I remembered yesterday, that she gave me a photograph album for safe-keeping. I found it buried in my craft room, another one of those items I need to get round to looking at. Anyway, here, look, she photographed everything, just in case anything went missing. There's even a note to go with it.'

Jenny read the note.

Life has a way of getting in the way of our plans. So, just in case, I have photographed all the items for Jenny's birthday treasure hunt.

'I didn't look at the album at the time, I wanted to see them for the first time when you got them.'

'Gosh, she was a canny old bird, wasn't she?' Jenny poured over the photographs. Everything she'd found was there. The Faberge Egg was beautiful. It looked like it was a very pale blue with a diamond trellis decoration covering it. The hen in the basket, was very much like the wren salts, though the hen was coloured. The gold plate was the size of a tea plate inscribed with words from the Tsar to his wife. 'Wow, I wish I'd seen it, in the flesh.'

'It is my sincerest wish, Jenny, that you get to do that someday soon;' said the Detective. 'I have alerted all of the auction houses who would deal with artefacts like these, and should anything be brought to them, they will let me know. I will do all I can, Jenny to see your items restored to you.'

'Thank-you Detective, I really appreciate all you are doing.'

'Oh yes, nearly forgot. We found a red fiesta on waste ground near Great Barr, registered to Michael Black. It looked like someone had tried to torch it, but weren't successful.'

When the Detective had left, Jenny opened the bag he'd given her. It was Michael's watch, but the ring, puzzled her. She'd found his ring in his bag with his laptop. This wasn't Michael's ring.

CHAPTER EIGHTEEN

The funeral was set for 22nd February at 12.45pm. Derek Allen took the service at the crematorium which was attended by Jenny, her parents, Jane Allen, DI Barnes, and Dana along with Jim and Robert Carruthers who were escorted by prison staff. Jenny tried not to look at them, but her eyes kept returning to them trying to see if there was any family resemblance between them and Michael; there was none that she could see. Jim sat with his head bowed, whilst Robert, looked all about him, grinned at Jenny and winked; and took the whole event as a day out. The service was short, no hymns and not a lot said by Derek. The music choice, she had left with Derek; something not too mournful, just nice. Jenny had wanted to give Michael some sort of service, but she didn't want to eulogise over a marriage that was so painfully a sham.

Derek read the commendation 'Let us commend Michael to the mercy of God, our maker and redeemer.'

Jenny felt numb as she listened to the words. 'Would God show his mercy to Michael?' she wondered.

'We have now entrusted our brother Michael to God's mercy, and now, in preparation for burial, we give his body to be cremated.'

'Well I guess that's one version of hell, that he'll experience.' Jenny thought to herself. She remained seated while everyone filed past the coffin on their way out.

'Do you want me to stay with you?' Jenny's mother asked her.

'No, I'm fine thanks mum. I just want a last moment.'

Jenny watched her mother leave, then stood up and walked over to the coffin which was waiting to roll through the doors to its fate.

'Well Michael, it's just you and me here now. You played me well. I fell head over heels in love with you, and you, you just wanted my inheritance. I've realised over the last fifteen months, that I can cope without you. I missed you terribly, but I coped. Sadly, I think you've got what you deserve, and I'm glad that I never have to set eyes on you again. I'm not sure I can wish you to rot in hell, but I do hope your afterlife is not pleasant. Bye Michael.' She pressed her fingers to her lips and briefly touched the coffin before walking out into the sunshine. She smiled at her parents and walked past Jim and Robert without looking at them.

'Thank-you Derek for the service.'

'You're welcome Jenny. I do pray that God may give you his comfort and peace.'

'I do too, Derek. I'm trying to forget the last few years and especially the last couple of months. Jane, thank you for all your help.'

'Tch, Tch, dear, it was a pleasure to help you. If there's anything else we can help you with, please let us know. Are you going home now?'

'Yes, I'm selling the house, I can't continue to live there with all the memories that I made there.'

'Are you sure you don't want to come back with us Jen?' her father asked.

'No, I need to go back home. I'll be back in a couple of weeks to see you. Bye.'

Jenny hugged her parents and got in her car. This would be the first time she'd been back to the house since she left in mid-January.

It felt strange drawing up on her drive. Jenny looked at the house with sadness. It had been her home since she started working at the library, before she'd met Michael. She reflected on all the happy times she thought she'd had, but was resolved to sell the house and move away. In the front garden, the for-sale board had already gone up, the estate agents were coming the following morning to take internal photographs.

Jenny pulled the card out of her pocket that Michael had written the alarm code on. She opened the front door and was met with silence instead of the beeping sound she was expecting. She stepped back outside and looked up at the top of the house. There was no alarm box with flashing light, like other houses in the road had. Stepping back inside, she could see no sensors at ceiling height or a control box in which to enter the code. Jenny checked all the rooms, just in case there were censors in some of them.

'Unbelievable. No alarm system, another con.' She said to herself. She now wondered if there were security cameras installed, but how would she know. She decided to call a security company once she'd unpacked her car.

Once unpacked, including a food parcel from her mother,

Jenny made herself a coffee and plugged in her laptop and entered internal security cameras in the search engine. The images that came back showed that they would look something like the non-existent alarm sensors. There was a plop as her post landed on the mat. It never failed to amuse her that her post nearly always arrived after lunch, though this was gone the middle of the afternoon. She wandered through to the hall and picked up her mail. She had asked the post office to redirect her letters to her parents for a month, resuming today. 'Well something works for once' she thought to herself. There was a large white envelope with a London post-mark. She took it back through to the kitchen and opened it. It was a letter from a Government department passing on their condolences.

Dear Mrs Black, please accept our most heartfelt condolences for the loss of your husband. Michael was one of our most valued operatives and for him to have sacrificed his life in service for others is commendable. As Michael lost his life while in service, you are the beneficiary to his pension. Please find attached a cheque for a lump sum. A monthly payment will be set up on receipt of your sort code and bank account number. If there is anything I can do to be of help, please do not hesitate to contact me. I remain your most humble servant, James Cardew.

Jenny looked at the second sheet of paper, it was a cheque for one hundred thousand pounds. She was glad she was sitting down, she felt as if her limbs had turned to jelly.

'Oh my goodness. Really, wow...' Jenny was amazed. The organisation perhaps didn't realise the circumstances Michael had died in, or were covering it up. 'I guess it wouldn't do to admit an agent had gone rogue' she said to herself. She dialled the number given in the letter.

'Hello, my name is Jenny Black...'

'Ah yes, Mrs Black, my sincerest condolences. This must be a trying time for you.'

'Yes, yes it is. Is that Mr Cardew?'

'My apologies, yes it is. What can I do for you Mrs Black?'

'Well, I know this sounds silly, but just after Christmas, Michael put in a security system in the house for my safety. Well, I've looked security systems up on the internet, but I can't find anything like it in the house.'

'Would you like one of our team to come and remove it for you? I'm guessing that he put in a hidden camera system.'

'If you could please, I'd be very grateful. I'm putting the house up for sale and I wouldn't want whoever bought it to have a shock.'

'No, of course not. I'll organise that for you, not a problem. Is there anything else I can help you with?'

'Um, err, yes, you asked for my bank details. Can I give you them now?'

Jenny gave the details to Mr Cardew and ended the conversation. Next, she rang Dana.

'Hi Dana, it's Jenny, I hope you don't mind me ringing and that I'm not interrupting anything, but you did say anytime.'

'Hi Jenny, it's not a problem. What can I do for you?'

'I have the photographer from the estate agent coming tomorrow morning, which in itself is not a problem. However, someone from the government office that Michael worked for will be coming to remove a hidden camera system, and I would really value you being here while they visit.'

'Ok, not a problem at all. I can come down this evening if you like, then I'll be there for whatever time someone shows up.'

'Would you really? That would be great. What time shall I expect you?'

'Looking at my watch, I can be with you by nine o'clock.'

'Lovely, thank you so much Dana, I really appreciate it.'

Having finished their conversation, Jenny prepared her meal. She plugged Michael's laptop in and opened it up. It was password protected. Jenny typed in the password he'd used prior to disappearing. M1ch43lBl4ck. Not a difficult password, but it worked. She looked at the file menu and spotted one that said Home.

'Not very imaginative Michael, is it' Jenny said out loud.

Each file was saved as a date. She turned to the dates when she was at her parents over Christmas. 23 12 15 showed Jenny clearly, packing and getting ready to leave. 26 12 15 was more surprising, it showed the intruder who picked up her post and place it on the coffee table. Whoever it was kept their head down, but as they turned to leave the room, lifted up their head and smiled. It was Oliver.

The love Jenny once had for Michael was transforming

itself into dislike and hate. He'd lied, not once, not twice, but many times.

The doorbell rang at 8.45pm. It was Dana, complete with a bottle of Pinot Grigio.

'Welcome, thank you so much for coming down.'

'Thank-you Jenny, and like I said it's no problem. I'm available to you for the duration of the case and quite possibly a little beyond it. Hope you like Pinot, I felt I couldn't arrive empty-handed. I even found a chilled bottle at the supermarket in their chillers.'

'Love it,' Jenny laughed 'come on in and get comfy, and I'll fetch a couple of glasses from the kitchen. Leave your bag in the hallway, then make yourself at home, first door on the right.'

They sat chatting while working their way through the entire bottle of wine before moving on to a whisky, until one in the morning. They mostly chatted about each other's jobs and what had made them follow their respective career paths.

Jenny was rudely awoken by the door-bell at half past

seven. She grabbed her dressing-gown and put it on while making her way downstairs managing to tie the sash as she opened the door.

'Good morning Miss,' came a bright and cheery voice 'I'm here from Mr Cardew to remove a little hardware that has been left.'

Jenny looked at him in amazement, how could anyone be that cheerful at this time of the morning. 'Right... ok... hello... well you'd better come in. You're very early aren't you?'

'S'pose so, not much traffic about early in the morning, so I can get the job done, get home ready for the footie this afternoon.'

'Well you'd better start in here' said Jenny, showing him the living room 'I know there was something in here. By the way, do you check phones as well?'

'Yes, no problem. It won't take long. Don't s'pose I could have a cuppa could I? Been a long drive.'

'No, that's ok, I need to put the kettle on any way. Tea or coffee?'

'Tea please, strong, two sugars and a good splash of milk. Name's Bert.'

'Hello Bert, well, I'll put the kettle on, and I'll be back with a drink for you.'

As Jenny came out of the living room, Dana came down the stairs, dressed.

'He's early isn't he?'

'Yes, bit of a shock to the system. Just going to put the kettle on he wants strong tea, two sugars and milk, just in case I'm not back down to make it.'

'That's ok, I'll sort him out.'

Jenny remembered she'd left Michael's laptop out on the kitchen table and followed Dana to the kitchen to pick it up.

'This should be charged by now,' she said, picking it up and unplugging it 'I'll take it back upstairs with me.' It wasn't that she didn't trust Dana, just the opposite, she just didn't know what else she might find stored on it.

Jenny returned downstairs, dressed, just as the kettle

finished boiling. Dana was on her way out of the living room as Jenny got to the kitchen. They'd agreed to make sure that they left Mr Cardew's man on his own for the least possible amount of time.

'It's ok Dana, I'll get the tea. Do you want tea or coffee?'

'Tea please, splash of milk and a half spoon of sugar. Thanks.'

Jenny carried the drinks through to the living room where she sat down opposite Dana and watched Bert work. He held what he called a detection wand in his hand which he waved over various items in the room. There were three cameras, set in a triangle to capture as much as possible going on in the room. They were all wireless, with a tiny transmitter attached to them and placed where Jenny would never have thought it possible to hide such an instrument. One was actually in the control panel of the DVD recorder, another wedged between books and the third behind the settee, in the picture frame. The telephone yielded a bug, as did the lamp in the corner of the room.

'Did you know that they're still active?'

'Really?'

Jenny and Dana shared a look of amazement.

'Well it was till I removed it.' Bert laughed. 'They've been here for a while too, at least a year. That's this room clear,' said Bert taking a slurp of his tea 'which room next?'

That meant Michael had put them in place long before he disappeared. They moved on to the dining room which Jenny rarely used. There was one camera hidden in there diagonally opposite the door. They moved on to the kitchen.

'Don't s'pose I could have another cuppa could I, that one was lovely.'

'Yes of course, would you like some toast as well?' Jenny asked.

'Ooohh, if you don't mind, thanks.'

'I'll do the toast and tea' said Dana, 'you carry on watching.'

Bert found two cameras in the kitchen and a bug in the phone before sitting down to tea and toast, neither of which hung around for long.

'Have you got any more rooms down here?' Bert asked.

'Just a downstairs loo under the stairs.'

Bert opened the door and waved the detection wand around the small space. 'All clear' Bert informed Jenny 'now we'd better check upstairs, just in case.

Jenny and Dana followed dutifully behind Bert. The smallest bedroom which was used for storage, had no cameras. Neither did the spare room that Dana had used. In Jenny's room, Bert found four cameras, which even he thought was a bit over the top.

'Perhaps he wanted to make sure I didn't have any male visitors' Jenny whispered to Dana.

The bedroom phone also had a bug. The bathroom had one camera which pointed at the door.

'Well at least he didn't watch me showering.' Jenny murmured.

'Any more rooms up here? Attic?' Bert asked.

'Yes, there's an attic, would there be anything up there?' Jenny asked.

'Better check and make sure.' Bert replied.

Jenny pressed a switch on the wall. Suddenly the attic hatch opened and a ladder unfurled itself ready for access. As the ladder reached the floor a light turned on in the attic space.

'Nice bit of kit, that'. Bert commented.

Bert climbed the steps and called down to Jenny and Dana.

'You might want to come up here and have a look.'

All three of them stood in the attic space and looked around them. There was a doorway through to the adjoining house.

'Jenny, did you know that was there?' Dana asked.

'No, I never came up to the attic, well not often anyway, when I did, it was for the Christmas tree and decorations, which as you can see are sat here next to the stairs. I don't think I'd have seen the doorway over there from the hatch and I'm pretty sure it wasn't there when I moved in.'

'I think we ought to go back down, and I'll call DI Barnes.' Said Dana.

Back down on the ground floor, Jenny thanked Bert for all his help and offered him another cup of tea, which he turned down.

Having said goodbye to Bert, Dana rang DI Barnes and informed him of what they had just found.

'He'll be here within the hour' she said 'meanwhile, I think we're in need of another cuppa.'

'Thank-you Dana, I don't think I've drunk so much tea in such a short time' Jenny smiled.

'Do you know your neighbours, Jenny?'

'No, the house has been mostly empty for as long as I've lived here. Apparently the chap who owns it works overseas and only comes back occasionally. Michael did meet him a couple of times. He said he was not really the friendly type. I've never seen him, though he's had a lot of building work and redecoration in the last six or so months. There was a builder's van then a decorator's van here for quite a while over that summer. I'm guessing now that some of that building work was gaining access to my attic.'

'Did Michael tell you the name of your neighbour?'

'No, I don't think he did. Just said he was a grumpy so'n'so and to stay away from him when he was around.'

'I'll check the electoral roll to see if we can find a name. Jenny, I'm afraid it might get a little busy round here for a few days, are you ok with that?'

'Oh, ok, no that's fine. Do you want me to stay here, or shall I go back to my parents?'

'Probably stay here, for now. DI Barnes said he was going to bring a search warrant for the house next door. If you'll excuse me, I'm going to get into detective mode, I think we have some work to do.'

'Is there anything I can do?' Jenny asked.

'Yes, try and stay relaxed and not worry too much. We'll get to the bottom of all this.'

Half an hour later, DI Barnes arrived with some news. 'The name of the person listed on the electoral roll is one Mr Simon Pellham, sound familiar?'

DI Barnes looked bemused as he shared this information with Jenny and Dana.

'You mean that son-of-a-bitch was living next door before we were married and then in the last few months.' Raged Jenny, 'If he wasn't already dead, I'd kill him, the bastard.'

'Unbelievable, not unheard of, it's quite rare. It is quite likely that although he owned the property, Michael rented it out.' Added Dana.

'Why didn't he tell me he owned the house? Why keep it on when he was living here with me?'

'Like I said if he was letting it out, then it was extra income. But strange he didn't tell you. Did you never visit his home before you were married?' Dana asked.

'No, he said he was renting a room in someone's house, so it never felt right going there. Can I see inside the house next-door?' Jenny asked.

'Not at present, Jenny. I have a team going through it room by room, floor by floor. We will cover every inch of it. The first job is to check for cameras and bugs, just in case it's all being recorded by anyone. I think as we're going to be spending a bit more time in each other's company, you can call me Stuart. DI Barnes, or Detective is getting a bit of a mouthful.'

'Thank-you Stuart. I have something upstairs that I think you and Dana should see. It's Michael's laptop. He left it at mums, so I brought it back with me. It has recordings of what he saw on the security cameras, and there is probably a whole lot of other stuff. I haven't had time to look through it.'

Jenny retrieved the laptop from her bedroom and gave it to Stuart, along with the password.

'Davies' Stuart called 'come in here, I have some work for you to do.'

A young PC came through to the kitchen.

'Davies, I want you to work with Dana here and see what is on this computer. Do not disregard anything. I want a full report as soon as possible.'

Jenny wandered through to the living room and looked out of the bay window. She wondered what the neighbours in the street thought with all the police action that was going on. There were police cars and forensic vans parked in front of the house and across the road. There was even a dog unit.

The phone rang. It was Jenny's mother.

'Hi Jen, have you settled back in ok?'

'Hi mum, yes, sort of. I had someone round to check for hidden security cameras and bugs, and we found a doorway in the attic to the house next door. The police have found out that Michael owned the house, under one of his aliases. He must have lived there before we got married, and possibly in the last few months. Mum, this is never-ending, I dread to think what they're going to find next door.'

'Are you having me on, love, I mean, surely you saw your neighbours?'

'No, I never saw them at all. I heard them occasionally. Mum he had cameras everywhere watching my every move. What sort of person does that?'

The doorbell rang.

'There's someone at the front door. I'll ring you back later, love you.'

Jenny opened the front door to find the photographer from the estate agents come to take the internal photographs.

'Er, Miss Bird?'

'Yes'

'Kevin Morris, Photographer from Moss and Crawley.'

'Oh yes, I was expecting you, please come in.'

'Are you sure it's convenient? There's a lot of police action out there'

'Yes, its fine, please come in and take your photo's. There are police here, but they're just working. If anyone is in the way, I'm sure they'll move while you take the photos.'

'I won't be long, if you want to walk round with me and check each photo as we go, I'll get them set up on the web page for you by tomorrow.'

'Stuart, Dana, this young man is here to take the photos for my house portfolio, he won't be here long.' Jenny felt she needed to explain to everyone who he was.

'These photo's are great. I think the only one I'm not sure of is the kitchen. Could you retake that one please.'

'Sure, no problem. I've got all the internal measurements. Do you want to see the blurb before it goes live?' the photographer asked.

'Um, it's a bit hectic here. Post it all online, when I manage to get a look, I'll let you know if anything needs changing. Just put some sort of disclaimer in so people don't sue you for misrepresentation.'

The afternoon slowly turned to evening. There was still activity next door. Stuart said they would continue in shifts until every inch had been looked at. PC Davies went off shift leaving Dana to continue going through the laptop. He'd be back early in the morning.

'Jenny, Dana will be staying with you for the next few days. I don't want you here on your own. There are officers next door still working and I will leave a car on patrol down the road keeping observation. Now you two need to eat, I'll go to the take-away for you, just let me know what you'd like. It's all on expenses.'

It took three days for the next-door house to be checked. Jenny was asked to look over a number of items that had been found, all in plastic evidence bags, the first of which, was the photograph taken from her wedding album. Jenny took hold of the bag and stared at the picture.

'It was in a frame, that was on the floor with the glass broken.'

Jenny looked at Dana.

'Michael told me categorically that he hadn't removed it. Another lie?'

She didn't recognise any of the other items that had been bagged.

Dana was writing up her report on what she had found on Michael's laptop when Stuart appeared in the kitchen. Jenny's home was now operating as an extension to the police station.

'Well, this has been a very interesting exercise indeed' Stuart began. 'It would appear that there were three people living in the property, all men. Whether they were all there at the same time, I wouldn't like to say. What we have found is a very comprehensive list of items they have stolen or purchased and of wanted items. I don't think, Jenny, you'll be surprised to hear that most of the items your great, great, grandmother was given, are on the list. The house would appear to have been used as the base for all their activities. There are catalogues from all the major auction houses, going back several years. Part of the attic looks like it was used as a photographic studio, the rest has ports for plugging in computers, printers and all sorts of equipment.'

'What about the door through between the two houses?' Jenny asked.

'Locked and bolted from their side, so even if you had found it, you wouldn't have been able to gain entry.'

'But why put a doorway through anyway?'

'Jenny, that I have no reasonable answer for, except that it would have allowed Michael, or whoever to have gained access to this side when you were at work or away without arousing the interest of your other neighbours. Your attic ladder works from the attic as well as the landing, allowing anyone in the attic to gain access to the rest of the house.'

'I guess that answers how the two Christmas cards got mixed up in my post and how Oliver gained entry…Is there any indication of when someone was last in there?'

'There are newspapers for the dates when you said Michael was back here putting in the security cameras and alarm. There is milk in the fridge, but it's well out of date judging by the colour of it alone. Though I did find an empty sandwich packet with a best before date for tomorrow, which indicates that someone has been in there very recently.'

'Do you think they left when they saw the hidden cameras being removed? Bert said they were still active.'

'It could well be, Jenny, and certainly if they saw us lot arrive.'

'So, do you think Michael and Ollie came back here after they left Wartlington on the bike?'

'I think at least one of them did, we found the plastic wrapping you described that would have been wrapped around your unopened parcel, the one that was stolen, and twenty-first birthday wrapping paper but I don't think they were here for long. One of the rooms had been turned over, drawers out of every piece of furniture, the bed was on its side and there were clothes thrown everywhere. None of the other rooms were found in this condition.'

'Do you know whose room it was?'

'No, there were no personal effects in any of them.'

Dana coughed politely 'would you like to hear what I've found on the computer?'

'Yes and No' Jenny replied.

'It would appear that the security cameras that were here in your home Jenny, were all motion activated, which is helpful when going through them. I can see that your home was entered on a number of occasions when you were out during the last year. There are also recordings of your telephone conversations, both from your landline and your mobile. But, what is most interesting, is a journal kept of all the actions taken by Michael and his brothers.'

CHAPTER NINETEEN

Dana handed Jenny a USB flash drive. 'I've copied the journal on to this for you Jenny. I think you should read it. The laptop will need to be bagged as evidence.'

'We're beginning to see that these four, or certainly two of these brothers were jewel thieves, in the widest sense of that description. They targeted items that had belonged to the Russian Imperial Family. We have connected them to a number of unsolved crimes across Europe. One of their mistakes was to leave their list behind or not destroy it. What we don't know, is where they stored goods until they disposed of them through the auction houses.'

'Thank-you Dana for the pen drive. Stuart, you don't suppose they used my side of the attic to store items, do you?'

'I was coming to that next. Jenny, do we have your permission to search your home? I will get a search warrant, if I have to, but having your permission will save a lot of hassle.'

'Yes, of course, please do search. I have nothing to hide, you know that. I feel like I'm living in a nightmare that has no end.'

'Thank-you Jenny. You are handling this very well. I've known some people in similar circumstances reduced to quivering wrecks. You're stronger than you give yourself credit for. I would like you to remain present while the search is going on. I don't want you thinking we've planted anything.' Stuart smiled sympathetically.

'I am a quivering wreck. I'm not sure how I'm coping with all this, though the support you and Dana are giving is helping tremendously.'

The search was more intrusive than Jenny had thought to imagine. All walls were checked for cavities. The gas fire was removed to check the flue. Carpets were pulled up along with floorboards. The kitchen cabinets were all emptied and checked. The downstairs toilet had a false wall that backed on to the stairs. This was removed.

'Sir, I've found something in here' a voice called from the toilet area.

Stuart looked in. 'Smarmy bloody fucking bastards …'

Jenny and Dana both looked at him, then took their turn

looking at what lay behind the wall. It was an A4 piece of paper with printed words on it that read 'COLD, REALLY COLD.'

'What does that mean?' Jenny asked, puzzled.

'It means, that they knew if we caught on to them, we would search both houses. Clever little sods. They are not going to get away with this any longer.'

'So it is likely that they used my home to hide their loot?' Jenny was horrified.

'Are you alright, Jenny?' Dana asked. 'You look very pale, come back to the kitchen and I'll make you a drink.'

Jenny sat down at the table, shaking her head in disbelief. 'I've made a decision. As soon as I can, I'm moving out. The house will have to sell when it's empty. I can't stay here any longer. I'm finding it very hard to accept that the man I loved and married, could do this to me…'

Dana had arranged for a sweep up team to follow round the house, putting everything back in order as soon as the search team had finished with a room. The downstairs loo was being treated as a crime scene, with forensics taking fingerprints and photographs. The A4 paper was removed from the wall and bagged.

Jenny plugged the flash drive into her laptop and read through the journal. None of the entries were dated.

Fallen in love with the woman I'm going to marry, not that she knows yet.

Jim will organise a speed-dating evening at his pub in the city. Fingers crossed.

Speed-dating successful. Moved in with the most wonderful woman.

It made Jenny smile when she remembered back to the days after the speed-dating. Michael had brought flowers every evening. By the end of the following week, her home was beginning to look like a florist's shop.

I'm getting married in the morning. Ding dong the bells are gonna chime...

Jenny remembered Michael had sung this almost all day long the day before they married. It drove her mad.

Cardew reassigning me. He's not happy. Nor am I.

Still can't bring myself to tell Jen that I own the house next door, even though Robbie is renting it off me. Told Jen neighbours not that nice, so she'll keep away.

Cardew putting pressure on.

Camera's now hidden in Jen's rooms, I can now see her everyday

Got to go undercover in Europe. Going to have to disappear. Wish I could have told Jen first, but not possible. Breaking my heart.

As Jenny read the words she felt as if the world had stopped turning. The noise from the forensic teams searching through her house faded into the background. She read the last three words again.

Breaking my heart.

'Not as much as it broke mine' Jenny thought. 'Michael, why couldn't you tell me. How terrible would it have been?' Tears rand down her face as she continued reading.

Mission is to follow a lead in Russia. Bloody freezing.

Don't believe it, tag is my brother, Ollie.

'So at this point, he must have been working legitimately.'

Jenny thought, 'I wonder if it was meeting or seeing Ollie that turned him?'

Jenny found the fact that Michael had three brothers totally at odds with what he'd told her. He was left orphaned, an only child, after his parents died in a speed-boat accident. Brought up by his grandmother who died the year before they'd met. Thus, there was no-one from his family to come to the wedding. So even back then, he'd lied to her.

Got Ollie on his own. Told him I was on holiday, and bumped into him outside the Kremlin. Said he was working in the archives recording the treasures from the days of the Russian Imperial family. Talked for ages over a meal and a few drinks. Interesting stuff. Money to be made. Spent a further couple of days with him. He's persuaded me that we can make money out of the treasures, while still working in our jobs. Told him to get in touch in a couple of weeks' time, when I'm back home.

Ollie wants to meet. He's left Russia with a copy of the inventory of missing items. Back in the UK for a few days. We are now both shacked up in the house next door. He thinks it's funny that I live next door to my wife who thinks I'm probably dead.

Ollie found diaries and letters from granny CC. There is a link to the Romanov family. Research on family tree shows pot of gold at rainbow's end. Ties in with the letter Jen found from her great, great, grandmother's parents.

Not sure I can go through with this. Jen's family is involved, and I've hurt her enough. Ollie says she probably doesn't know about any of the treasures. He's probably right, she's never mentioned them.

'So he did love me? God this is so confusing. If he didn't want to hurt me, why did he carry on? What a bastard.'

Jim now landlord of pub in Wartlington.

Building and decorating work finished. House quite habitable now that Robbie has moved out.

We need more information on the older generations of the family. Time to come back from the dead.

'So he came back to find out what I knew or what I'd got?'

Jenny stared at the screen shaking her head in disbelief.

Ollie and I have travelled all over Europe and been amazed at the number of things we've traced that had gone missing. Selling them at auctions has been a doddle.

Still in love with Jen, not sure I can do this to her anymore. Ollie agreed it will be our last job.

'But you didn't bloody well stop, did you?'

The journal entries left Jenny as perplexed as ever. Michael loved her, yet could still steal her inheritance. Unbelievable.

Robbie is new tenant at the farm. Heaven help us all.

Not sure I trust Ollie.

This was the last entry. If Ollie had shot Michael, then dumped his body on the motorway, then Michael's intuition had been working well, Ollie was not to be trusted.'

A call came from upstairs. Jenny and Dana went up and met Stuart on the landing.

'None of the bedrooms or the bathroom have anything. However, the attic. Well the attic has been used for storing items before being sold on. Come on up.'

Jenny and Dana followed Stuart up the attic steps. Along the side of the partition between the two houses were black bin bags containing packaging materials, labels and storage boxes. Opening up one of the boxes, revealed another A4 paper with an emoticon smiley face with the words

TOO DAMN LATE

CHAPTER TWENTY

Thursday 22nd June 2017 was memorable for its weather. The hottest day on record since 1976. Jenny and Dana sat in the auction house thankful for the air-conditioning keeping the heat at bay. They were not sat together. They, along with Stuart Barnes were dotted about amongst the people gathered to bid on the largest array of goods from the Romanov family found in the last twenty years. Sat among the bidders, were Jenny's parents and Derek and Jane Allen. Both Derek and Philip had been dressed up to look like oligarchs while Eloise, Jenny's mother and Jane had been dressed up to the nines as the glamorous wives. None of them had acknowledged any of the others. They were all registered to bid.

There were two aisles of chairs facing the back wall of the room. The back wall had an auctioneers desk in the middle and was flanked by a huge monitor to its left side and a smaller screen set on a white background to its right. In front of the screen on the left was a long desk behind which stood ten gentlemen in suits, each in charge of a telephone connected either to an operative on the computer or clients.

The catalogue was beautifully printed with colour

photographs of each lot and a generous description. The sale was titled 'Treasures of the Romanov Family.'

Jenny had reserved her seat and stood at the back of the hall watching people as they came in. She was watching for a particular face, but so far, it hadn't appeared. A couple of plain-clothes policemen were also on watch duty.

There was a palpable buzz of excitement in the room as people examined pictures of the featured lots. As the auctioneer entered the hall conversations ceased.

'If I could ask everyone to take their seats and to ensure that your mobile phones are switched off, we will begin.'

The first lot was a pair of salts, not dissimilar to the wrens that Jenny owned. People in the seats would bid and now and then one of the gentlemen on the phones would nod in the direction of the auctioneer indicating a bid. It was a very sedate affair. The auctioneer was gently spoken, but with a voice that lulled you into wanting to bid. Each lot was captured by a camera and shown on large screens enabling every detail to be seen. Many of the items brought admiring gasps from the bidders.

'Sold to the lady in the white hat, thank you Madam. Next

we have lot number 108…'

This was the gold plate. There was a bidding frenzy until finally the auctioneer announced, 'Sold to the gentleman on the front row' and bowed to him.

The auction was now half way through. There was a slight disturbance at the back of the hall, which, when Jenny turned around, showed to be an elderly lady, whose walking stick had slipped on the floor, causing her to stumble. The Auction room staff were quick to attend her. Jenny noticed Stuart Barnes had left his seat, but couldn't see where he'd gone. The auction continued.

'And now to our final piece. I'm sure you will agree it is a fine piece of workmanship by the famous Carl Faberge. Thought to be the second egg given to Empress Maria Feodorovna by her husband the Tsar Alexander III in 1886, it is known as the Hen with Sapphire Pendant or the Egg with Hen in Basket. Thought to have been missing since the Russian Revolution, a copy was uncovered in the Kremlin Archives. I open the bidding at 1.3 million pounds. Thank-you sir. 1.4 with me… 1.5, 1.6 with me…'

The bidding continued to twenty-three million. Jenny felt her heart pounding in her chest.

'Sold to the lady in the white hat. Congratulations Madam.'

Jenny stood up and acknowledged the applause. 'Oh my God, I've just purchased my own egg.' She murmured under her breath. There was a sudden commotion at the back of the hall. Jenny turned round and saw Stuart wrestling the old lady to the floor. She didn't see anything else, as by the time she'd focussed on him properly, the whole contingent of bidders was on its feet. She moved from her seat and met with her parents and Derek and Jane Allen. Dana found her after a few minutes and passed on the news that they had arrested Oliver Carruthers.

Jenny walked over to the auctioneer and was led to the back rooms to meet with the Executive Officer. He presented her with her plate and egg. Jenny stared at the egg. It was beautiful and so delicate. She found it hard to believe that it actually belonged to her. She held it in both hands afraid of what would happen to it if she dropped it.

'Miss Bird, it gives me the greatest pleasure to return your items to you. It has been a most successful afternoon as I hear that the perpetrator has been arrested. You will also be pleased to know that most the items have been traced back to their owners; there are going to be a number of people thankful to you and the police team.'

'Thank-you Mr Smith. What you have done today has been absolutely amazing. I did have a lot of fun spending money I don't actually have, though it was very nerve-racking.'

'We were only too happy to help. When the Police Commissioner came to me with the plan, I must say I was sceptical. We have never ever run a false sale before. I must also add that I hope we do not have to run one again. It was, to use your phrase, nerve-racking indeed.'

'Excuse me for asking, Mr Smith, but how did you manage not to actually sell any of the items given the number of people who were here?'

'There were only ten people we were actually accepting bids from so that we could control it. We kept accepting higher bids until it was one of the ten who were the top bidders. Mr Bennet, the auctioneer did a marvellous job selling items that were not for sale. Should you ever wish to sell your items, please do contact us, we will be only too happy to attend to your sale.'

Jenny met with Dana and Stuart a few days later to thank them and say goodbye, though she was sure she'd see them again when the case came to court.

'How did you know that the old lady was Ollie?' Jenny asked.

'Well, while he did a pretty good job falling when his walking stick slipped, most old ladies I know don't have a five o'clock shadow or sit with their legs so wide apart you could drive a bus through them. He must have been finding the wig a bit itchy, because PC Davies who was stood to the side of him, noticed he kept sticking his hand under the wig to scratch his head. Oliver Carruthers had obviously not studied how an old lady behaves. And unfortunately, every time the bids went up, he could be heard talking out loud to himself and at one point he punched the air. It wasn't too hard to see through his disguise.'

'How are you now Jenny?' Dana enquired.

'To be honest, I'm glad it's all over now. The house has sold, which I'm quite relieved about and until I find somewhere to buy, I'm staying with my parents. I gave up my job and I am currently what some of my friends describe as 'a lady of leisure'. The house next door has also been sold and the money given to charities that support victims of abuse. I want to thank you both for all the support and help you've given me over the last few months.'

'We were only doing our job, weren't we Dana. I'm glad we were able to help and get the whole problem resolved.'

The case came to court three months later. Jenny sat with Dana listening to the pre-amble of choosing a jury. When it came for the moment when Ollie was brought in, Jenny looked confused.

'Dana, who is that they've just brought in?

'Oliver Carruthers.'

'That's not Ollie. I don't know who he is, but he isn't Ollie. I have a photograph of him on a sim card.'

'Oh bollocks. Are you sure?'

'Yes, positive.'

'How could this mistake have happened? Bear with me Jenny, I'll be back in a few moments.'

CHAPTER TWENTY ONE

Dana left the court and sought out the court staff member outside. 'I need to get a message to the judge or the prosecution lawyer. It is urgent and paramount to this case.'

A few moments later, an official gave a message to the prosecuting team.

'Your honour, I seek a stay of proceedings.'

'Approach the bench.'

'Your honour, may I speak to you privately in your chambers? It is very important and will have an impact on this hearing.'

'Ok. It had better be good.'

Moments later, the lawyer was in the Judges chamber.

'What is it Mr Jenkins, you're not known for this sort of thing so it had better be good or I'll have you up for wasting court time.'

'Your honour it has just come to my attention that the accused is not Oliver Carruthers.'

'Repeat that please.'

'The accused is not…'

'That's what I thought you said. So, who exactly is he?'

'Well that's just it Your honour I'm embarrassed to say we don't know.'

'Tell me Jenkins, how is it you have managed to get this far in the whole proceedings to only find out now that you don't have the right man?'

'I don't know Your honour. He has never denied that he is Oliver Carruthers.'

'How do you know he is not Oliver Carruthers?'

'Mrs Black, the accused's sister in law.'

'Never in my whole career, have I come across such ineptitude. I have no choice but to go back out there and throw this case out.'

The judge picked up his phone and asked for the Defence counsel to come to his chambers.

'Thank you for coming, Mr Bentley. I have to ask you a

couple of questions.'

'Yes Your honour.'

'What is the name of your defendant?'

Bentley looked puzzled, but answered anyway. 'Carruthers, Your honour, Oliver Carruthers. May I ask why you are asking?'

'It has come to my notice that your defendant whom you know as Oliver Carruthers, is not Oliver Carruthers.'

Bentley stood open-mouthed in front of the Judge.

'I don't understand Your honour.'

'Just what exactly do you not understand?'

'That my client Oliver Carruthers, is not Oliver Carruthers, Your honour.'

I am going to have this case thrown out, but be warned that your defendant will not be released. I want him re-arrested and questioned about who he really is and why he is carrying this can for Carruthers.'

Dana returned to Jenny and explained what was happening.

'I've spoken to Stuart and he's ready to come in and arrest the man posing as Carruthers. We'll have to question him.'

The court clerk entered the court and spoke. 'All rise.'

The Judge addressed the court. 'It has come to my notice that evidence submitted for this case is being withdrawn. I am going to dismiss this case. However, the defendant will remain in custody. Case dismissed.'

Two hours later, the defendant known as Oliver Carruthers, was being questioned by DI Barnes.

'For the tape, please give me your name.'

'Oliver Carruthers.'

'Right sunshine. I am going to ask you again for your name and I warn you, I know you are not Oliver Carruthers, so I want your proper name. Do not waste my time.'

The man smiled.

'Ok you got me bang to rights. It's Fred Blakey.'

'Address?'

'Flat 3, Lancaster House, Bentley Street.'

Stuart Barnes left the room and returned fifteen minutes later having checked Fred Blakey's details.

'So, Mr Blakey, tell me why you posed as Oliver Carruthers.'

'This geezer came up to me in the pub and said he had a little job for me. He said I was to attend an auction and watch how much money was raised through sales. I was paid 'ansome like. The only proviso was, I had to dress as an old bird. Well if you're paid a few thousand, enough to keep you in fags and beer for a few years, it wasn't too bad a job. I've had worse, I can tell you. He said that if I was arrested I was to tell the rozzers that me name was Oliver Carruthers. He also said, that even if I went to court, the case would be thrown out so I wouldn't end up in prison. Looks like he was right don't it.'

'Unbelievable. Who was the person who approached you with this marvellous plan. Can you describe him?'

'Don't know his name. Didn't meet him for very long. He just said he'd been sent by a friend with a proposition. He was 'bout my age, dark hair, beard. When I agreed, he said the money would be put in my account in instalments. The first one arrived in me bank that night.'

Stuart sat shaking his head. How could they have messed this up?

'I need to check your bank account to see if further instalments have been made?'

'Ok Guv, I'd be interested to see if they have too.'

'Could you please write down your account details and I'll check for you. I'll print off a statement.'

Fred Blakey wrote down his bank details and passed the paper back to Stuart, who left the interview room to check the bank account. He returned half an hour later.

'Well Mr Blakey, it seems you are a very fortunate man, a couple of instalments were made beginning with the day you say you were approached. A second instalment was made the day you were arrested and three hours ago, a final instalment was made making you quite a wealthy man. You are now free to go, but please be aware if we need to, we will be back in touch.'

'You mean I can keep the money?'

'No your account is frozen. We will get these instalments removed while we carry out further investigations and then return your account to you.'

'Bugger. Knew it was too good to be true. Thanks Guv.'

Jenny was using the internet for her search for a new home when a message alert popped up on the task bar at the bottom of the screen. It was one of her Chums Online friends. As she opened up the message, she saw it was from Meredith. Her whole body froze as she read:

Hi hun, been away for a while, but I'm back now. Did you miss me?

CHAPTER TWENTY TWO

Jenny sat staring at the screen, not believing what she was seeing. Jenny's mother walked into the living room.

'Jen, whatever is the matter, you're as white as ghost.'

'Mum… come and look at this, tell me I'm not seeing things.'

'Meredith? Is this your friend who is, I mean was, Michael?'

'Yes… He's dead, so how…?

'We need to call Dana, love or that DI.'

'I'll take a screen-print and a photograph. What if he isn't dead? What if that wasn't Michael? What…'

'Let's leave it to the police, love. I'll go and ring them.'

Forty minutes later, Stuart Barnes was sat in the living room of Rose Cottage.

'What does this mean, is he still alive or what?'

'Jenny, I'm at a loss as to how to explain this. You identified Michael, as did we through his fingerprints.'

'When you gave me his personal effects, there was a wedding ring in the bag. I'm not sure it was Michael's. He left his ring upstairs with his laptop when he went.'

'Have you got them both? We can get them analysed.'

'Yes, I'll go and get them.'

Jenny returned moments later with both rings. 'This one is the one he left behind, it has the date of our wedding engraved inside it and this one is the one you gave me at the morgue which isn't engraved.

Stuart looked at both rings and placed them in evidence bags.

'Looking at them, I can't see any difference in them. They are identical. The lab will be able to tell us if they were worn by the same person or not.'

'I've been investigating the bank deposit made to Fred Blakey and our search brings us back to one account and that is in the name of Jennifer Black.'

Jenny gasped. 'You cannot be serious. I have one bank account only and it's in the name of Jennifer Bird, here…' Jenny fetched her bank card out of her purse. 'You can check it…'

'Jenny, I am not accusing you, but can you at any time, remember signing a bank book for Michael or opening an account with him?'

'No, no this doesn't make any sense. We kept our own bank accounts. We intended to open a joint account, but never got round to it.'

'Jenny, I need a sample of your handwriting. A sentence and a signature, and I'll get them analysed along with the signature that the bank holds for the account that has your name on it.'

'What do you want me to write?'

'Anything will do.'

Jenny wrote her parents address down on a piece of paper and added her signature. 'Is that ok?'

'Yes, thank you. Now, as regards this new message from Meredith. I can understand how unsettling this must be for you, but will you carry on the conversation with her, as if you don't know she's actually someone else? If I could have your account password and details, I will get a track on the account. It will take a couple of days to check your handwriting. Dana will be here very shortly. I would also like her to stay here with you, if that's ok with your parents.'

'Yes that's fine Mr Barnes, Philip and I are more than happy to have a police presence. We can introduce Dana as one of Jenny's university friends.'

'Thank-you Mrs Bird. Jenny, I'll be back to you in a couple of days.'

After Stuart Barnes left, Jenny returned to her laptop and the message she'd received from Meredith. She had no idea what to write, or even if she really wanted to. Stuart must have a reason for asking her to do this. Jenny was relieved when Dana arrived, as she didn't know how to continue or if she wanted to.

'Jenny, I'm going to log on as you on my laptop, if that's ok, and we'll continue this together and hopefully, we'll root out whoever is behind this. We just have to be careful with our questions and responses.'

Dana started typing a reply.

Hi Meredith, long time no hear, I thought perhaps you'd left the planet, lol. Have you been away somewhere nice?

Here and there, mainly Europe.

Sounds exciting, where did you visit?

Austria and Switzerland, just as beautiful in the summer as it is in the winter. How are you doing these days?

I'm fine, never better. Got my life back on track. How would you like to meet up, in the flesh, so to speak, rather than just on here? I'd love to finally meet you.

'Do you think whoever it is, will go for that?' Jenny asked.

'We'll find out, hopefully, in a minute.' Dana replied. They didn't have to wait long.

I guess we could, it would be lovely to meet you in the flesh, so to speak. How about London? I'm there now visiting a friend. If you could make it tomorrow, that would be great.

Tomorrow is fine. Where and when?

'Jenny, I think we've hooked them.'

How about Trafalgar Square underneath the people's plinth, say, 1pm?

Fine, looking forward to finally meeting you, see you tomorrow. Bye.

'Right, let's see if we can find out where the message was coming from.'

Dana tapped on a tab on her laptop that had been running while she was on Chums Online.

'OK, whoever it is was telling the truth, they are in London. PC Davies will be here tomorrow, just in case they use this visit as an excuse to come back here. Leave the arrangements with me and we'll see who Meredith really is.'

CHAPTER TWENTY THREE

The station concourse was busy. People were stood staring at the arrival and departure boards seemingly mesmerised by the changing information. Jenny followed Dana as she threaded her way through the groups of people to the underground. The platform was just as busy as the main station. It was hot and airless and having managed to get on a train found there was standing room only. They were both relieved to get off at Charing Cross and out into the fresh air. Here they only had to cross the road to Trafalgar Square. The people's plinth was in the top right hand corner of the square, behind Nelson's Column. A tourist bus had just deposited its passengers who were standing in small groups taking photographs of each other in front of the lions guarding the fountains. Jenny and Dana had left the tube station separately though Dana made sure that they were both wearing a microphone and ear-piece and had placed a tracker, unknown to Jenny, in her jacket pocket. Jenny made her way to the plinth and stood beneath it waiting for Meredith to arrive. She held tightly onto her bag with her arms folded and watched people feeding the pigeons.

'What a ridiculous thing to do, there's enough discarded

food on the ground as it is.' She murmured.

'Flying rodents, is what I call them.' Laughed Dana.

One woman who was throwing bird seed on the ground slowly made her way over to Jenny. She was wearing a red wig and sunglasses.

'Are you Jenny?' she asked.

'Yes. Meredith?'

'Yes and No. I've been asked to pass this envelope on to you.' She delved into a large shoulder bag.

'Sorry, did you say you were Meredith or not?'

'No, I've just been asked to be here to meet a woman, who looks like you and pass on this envelope.'

Unknown to Jenny, Dana and Stuart had arranged for local plain-clothed police to be in the area, in case anything went awry.

'Go, go, go, don't let the woman get away.' Dana ordered through her radio.

The woman thrust the envelope into Jenny's hand, said

goodbye, and walked towards the Art Gallery. She only made it to the steps behind the plinth before she was apprehended.

'Jenny, stay where you are, I'll come and meet you' Dana said through her microphone.

Jenny looked all about her, bemused by what had just happened. She had expected to see Michael or Ollie, dressed up as a woman or as themselves but instead, she had met a woman asked to deliver her an envelope. She opened it cautiously. Inside was a postcard of Trafalgar square with a poem written on the back.

How do I love thee? Let me count the ways.
I love thee to the depth and breadth and height
My soul can reach, when feeling out of sight
For the ends of Being and ideal Grace.
I love thee to the level of everyday's
Most quiet need, by sun and candle-light.
I love thee freely, as men strive for Right;
I love thee purely, as they turn from Praise.
I love thee with a passion put to use
In my old griefs, and with my childhood's faith.
I love thee with a love I seemed to lose

With my lost saints, --- I love thee with the breath,

Smiles, tears, of all my life! --- and, if God choose,

I shall but love thee better after death.

Tears stung her eyes. She felt her legs go to jelly and she leaned back against the plinth. She looked round for Dana, who she saw approaching her. Her mobile buzzed in her pocket. It was a text from her mother's phone.

'Hope you got the message, your parents are safe. No harm will come to them. All I want is the egg. Return to the plinth tomorrow, no later than 3pm with the egg and I will release them.'

'Aaaaaaaarrrrgggghhhhhhh'

Dana heard Jenny scream and ran the last few metres to her. People turned and looked at Jenny as she screamed then carried on as if nothing had happened. Dana's mobile buzzed. It was a text from Stuart.

Davies has been found unconscious at Rose Cottage. He's being taken to hospital with a suspected skull fracture. Jenny's parents have gone.

'Jenny, are you ok?'

'No, the bastard's got my parents. I thought you'd left a

policeman with them.'

'I did, that was Stuart letting me know that PC Davies has been found unconscious and your parents gone. What does the letter say?'

Jenny handed over the card.

'I have to get the egg; my parents are more important than some Russian trinket.'

'Where is the egg?'

'Here in London. I didn't know what to do with it, so it's in a safety deposit box, while I make a decision. Guess that's just been taken out of my hands.'

'We have the woman who handed you the envelope, she's being taken to the local nick and will be questioned. Are you sure, you want to do this?'

Jenny looked at Dana amazed that she'd asked such a question.

'What I mean is, do you really want to hand over the egg, and let Michael or whoever get away with it or can we devise some sort of plan?'

'Right at this moment, I don't care what we do, as long as my parents are released, unhurt.'

'OK, let's find somewhere to stay the night, then get down to sorting out a plan of action.'

They found a cheap hotel near Leicester Square and booked a room with twin beds. The hotel was not very modern, but it was clean and well kept. Dana was not going to let Jenny out of her sight. She rang Stuart Barnes to let him know what they were doing. He arranged to meet them at 8pm that evening. 'Jenny, have you given any thought to how you are going to package the egg?'

'No. I guess it would look odd passing it over in a carrier bag.'

'How about we nip along to the card shop we passed, down the street, and see if they have any gift boxes then to the casual observer, it will look like your delivering a present?'

'Sounds ok to me.'

Dana sent off a couple of messages on her phone before they went shopping.

By the time Stuart arrived at their hotel later that evening, they had formulated a plan. Stuart brought the news that Davies was out of theatre.

'A clot had formed on his brain and has been removed. Apparently he's stable but still very poorly. I also have news about your bank account. It is a second account, in your name, but having checked your handwriting against that held by the bank, I can confirm that your signature has been forged.'

'I have to say I feel a great relief to hear that. What about the rings?'

'The report says they have both been worn by the same person.'

'Why would he need two rings? That's just mad.'

'There's only one person can answer that for you.'

The next morning, just before noon, Jenny and Dana went to the bank where the egg was stored and returned to the hotel an hour later. Stuart arrived at the same time and handed over a small package to Dana.

'Thanks Boss. Hope it hasn't caused to much of a problem.'

'Nah, local boys are very good.'

'Right Jenny, let's get this show on the road. You have got this insured, haven't you?'

'Oh yes, costs a bomb.'

Dana opened up the parcel. Inside was the smallest tracking device Jenny thought it was possible to have. It wasn't a single one, there were about eight.

'Wow, they're so tiny.' She exclaimed.

'Yep, we don't want any of them to be seen. Now then, let's open up the egg and see what's inside.'

Opening the egg revealed the hen sat on its basket, which in turn opened to reveal a sapphire pendant.

'Right' said Dana picking up a pair of tweezers 'first one fitted just inside the pendant setting. Second one in the base of the basket. Clever of you Stu to get gold coloured ones. There's the pendant back in the basket.'

Dana made a note where each device was being placed.

'Third one on the inside of the hen. Fourth one inside the

egg.'

'Won't they all interfere with each other?' Jenny asked.

'No, they all have a unique code, which we can track. If any of the items get separated, it means we can track and find them. So, number five is going on the tissue paper, number six on the inside of the box, number seven on the inside of the lid and number eight, we'll see if we can deposit on whoever picks this beauty up from you.'

'This is very high-tech.'

'We want to retrieve your egg as well as have your parents released, Jenny.'

At 2.45pm Jenny left the hotel with the box wrapped in ribbon in her handbag. She was followed by Dana and Stuart, who left arm in arm, as if a couple. They crossed over to the other side of the street, so that to the casual observer, it didn't look as if they were following Jenny.

By 3pm, Jenny was stood back under the people's plinth. At 3.15pm, Jenny was getting worried that nobody was going to show after all. A voice spoke behind her, sending a cold shiver down her spine. It was Michael.

'I don't understand…' her words came out choked as she span round.

'Sorry to have to do this to you Jen, but my need is greater than yours. Hand over the egg, and I'll arrange to have your parents released by 3.30pm. I'm glad you came on your own. I was worried that you'd have your policewoman friend with you. Good girl for being brave.'

'I… thought you… were… dead. Tell me… whose body did I cremate?' Tears escaped.

'Ah, sadly, that was Ollie. We got into a fight, and he lost.'

'I really don't understand you Michael. He was your brother…how could you do this?' 'Quite easily, it appears.'

'I shared my life with you. Everything I had was yours, wasn't that enough?.. MICHAEL answer me. Help me understand.'

Michael took the box from Jenny. 'Stand still, while I make sure the goods are in the box.'

He undid the ribbon and took the lid off the box. Pulling the tissue paper back, he inspected the egg for the registration mark and its contents. Satisfied, he put it back in the box.

'Why couldn't you tell me you had brothers? In fact, why couldn't you just tell me the truth from the beginning? I loved you...'

'Thanks Jen, you're a star. I will now leave you in peace. Please stay here until 3.30pm, and you'll get your parents returned to you.'

'You're a right royal piece of work, aren't you? Complete and utter bastard does not do justice to how I really feel about you. I loved you. I though you loved me... what changed?'

'By the way, you were a good shot with the gun, at least I missed you, but you managed to get my arm.' He rubbed his right arm just above his elbow.

'WHY CAN'T YOU ANSWER MY QUESTIONS?'

He went to kiss her, but Jenny dodged the kiss, and grabbed his wrist with both hands. She managed to fix the last tracking device, which was magnetic, onto the side of his watch and then fended him off.

'Bye Jen. I did love you, you know. I still do.'

He walked away from her swinging the carrier bag in which he'd placed the box.

Jenny could hear Dana's voice in her earpiece.

'Well done Jenny. The troops on the ground will follow him, and we are following the tracking devices.'

'Where's he going, can you tell?'

'It looks like he's gone underground on the tube, the trackers will tell us where he is.'

Jenny looked around her not able to see through the haze of tears. 'Where are you, I can't see you?'

'Look at Nelson's column. Can you see the couple standing arm in arm under the column?'

Jenny wiped a hand across her eyes. 'Really, is that you two?'

'Yes, but don't read anything into it.'

Just after 3.35pm Jenny's phone rang.

'Hi Jen, it's us, we're at the police station, we've just been left here. Are you ok love?'

'Mum, I'm so glad to hear your voice. Are you ok?'

'Yes, we're fine, a bit shaken up, but otherwise…'

'He's alive. Michael's still alive and has just taken off with my egg… '

'Leave it to the Police, Jen, they'll sort it out. Are you coming back?'

I don't know when I'll be back, but I'll see you soon. Love you.'

Two police cars with sirens blazing went past the bottom of the square, followed by a third one a couple of minutes later.

'Dana, my parents are ok. They were left at a police station. What's happening now?'

'I'm waiting for an update. Can you make your way over here?'

'Just give me a minute or two.'

Jenny stood looking up at the sky and closed her eyes. She could feel the late summer sun warming her skin. She took a couple of deep breaths before walking over to Dana who put her arm around Jenny's shoulders.

'Jenny you did really well. All eight trackers are working. It looks like Michael is currently at London Bridge. Stuarts gone off to coordinate everything. I think you could do with a drink. There's a café just over the road, come on.'

'What about Michael?'

'We'll be kept up to date with all information. There's nothing more you can do now. Then we'll go back to the hotel.'

'Did you hear everything?'

'Yes, he was very evasive, wasn't he?'

'He didn't answer my questions. I really thought I knew him, but it seems I didn't know him at all.'

Dana checked her mobile. 'It looks like Michael left the tube at North Greenwich and is now in a car. How about we go back to the hotel, and see if Stuart has any news?'

Jenny smiled, stood up and hugged Dana.

'Thank you for being a friend. I'm really grateful for everything.'

Approaching the hotel, Jenny could see a police car with its lights flashing, outside the entrance. Jenny ran towards it as an officer got out of the car.

'Miss Bird, would you please come with us?'

Dana caught up with Jenny.

'Could I have a word with you officer, on your own please?' she asked, showing her badge and pulled him off to one side out of earshot of Jenny. 'What's going on?'

'There's been an accident.'

'One of our colleagues was following the tracking devices. It was going at some speed, so I guess the perp was in a car. Suddenly it stopped. When the officer got there, he found the car wrapped around a tree. Occupant dead at the scene.'

'Was the box intact?'

'Yes M'am. It's being taken to Scotland Yard. I was sent to

fetch Miss Bird.'

'Ok, I'll accompany her.'

Dana turned back to Jenny and walked over to her. 'There's been a development. We need to go with this officer, we'll meet Stuart at the station.'

At Scotland Yard, Jenny and Dana were shown through to an interview room. Stuart Barnes walked in five minutes later carrying the box with the egg in it.

Jenny looked at Stuart with apprehension.

'Jenny, I have good news and bad news. The good news is I can return your egg to you. The bad news… I'm sorry, Michael has lost his life.'

Jenny sat still, trying to take in what Stuart had said clutching the parcel to her. She tried to speak, but nothing came out. Dana asked the question for her.

'How did this happen, Stuart?'

'One of the cars we had on patrol put out a stinger, Michael ran over it, kept going but lost control of his vehicle. He was pronounced dead at the scene. The car is mangled around a tree.' He paused letting the news sink in. Big gulps were now escaping from Jenny to accompany the stream of warm tears cascading down her face. She leaned into Dana, allowing her to put her arms around her.

'I have news about the woman posing as Meredith. She was paid by Michael to bring you the envelope. She didn't know him. He apparently approached her a couple of days ago having got into a conversation with her in the coffee bar across the road from Trafalgar Square, and just like Fred Blakey, was paid well for her work.'

'Is he really d-d-dead this time? He's not likely to rise from the grave again is he?'

'Jenny, I can confirm he is deceased. We will need you to identify the body. I don't think there is any question this time that it is Michael. From the ticket I found in the car, it looks like he was on his way to Dover to catch a ferry to Ostend. Perhaps he thought he'd have better luck selling the egg abroad. If you want to unwrap the box, we'll remove the trackers now, while you watch. I've heard that your parents have been released.'

'Yes mum rang me. What about the policeman, is he is ok?'

'Out of danger and he'll be ok. I think he'll be in hospital for a while though.'

'If Michael was here in London, who…'

'That we're not sure about, probably someone who was paid to do the job. Michael would have contacts from his work. From what I can gather, Davies was attacked from behind and your parents were taken at gunpoint to the Priory before being driven to the local police station where they were released.' You are now free to get on with the rest of your life. I've arranged for a car to take you home. Dana is available to you, if you need her and she'll travel back with you.'

'Thank you, Stuart, I feel quite numb, but glad this is now finally over.'

ABOUT THE AUTHOR

Carol Kennedy lives with her husband who is the vicar of two rural parishes in North Warwickshire and have three grown up children. When not acting as carer for their middle child, who is autistic, she ran her own cross-stitch business, designing and producing charts and kits. The rest of her working life has been in administration and management, which includes a hospital in Toronto, Ontario, a Rural Community Council, a catalogue distribution company, a Christian Charity and a parish church.

Carol has a BA (Hons in Leadership and Management and an MA in English (with merit).

18345607R00201

Printed in Poland
by Amazon Fulfillment
Poland Sp. z o.o., Wrocław